AMARYLLIS

Also by Nikita Lynnette Nichols

None But The Righteous

A Man's Worth

AMARYLLIS

NIKITA LYNNETTE NICHOLS

www.urbanchristianonline.net

Urban Books
1199 Straight Path
West Babylon, NY 11704

Amaryllis copyright © 2009 Nikita Lynnette Nichols

ISBN- 13: 978-1-60162-986-9
ISBN- 10: 1-60162-986-9

First Printing April 2009
Printed in the United States of America

10 9 8 7 6 5 4 3 2 1

This is a work of fiction. Any references or similarities to actual events, real people, living, or dead, or to real locales are intended to give the novel a sense of reality. Any similarity in other names, characters, places, and incidents is entirely coincidental.

Distributed by Kensington Corp.
Submit Wholesale Orders to:
Kensington Publishing Corp.
C/O Penguin Group (USA) Inc.
Attention: Order Processing
405 Murray Hill Parkway
East Rutherford, NJ 07073-2316
Phone: 1-800-526-0275
Fax: 1-800-227-9604

Dedication

I wish to dedicate this novel to my priceless gems: Tabitha Renee, my Ruby; Toiya Raynae, my Sapphire; Tashea' Victoria, my Jade; William James II, my Topaz; and Kenneth Keith, my Diamond. Also, to my baby. He's my Onyx.

Acknowledgements

Now, unto *Him*, *Who* is able to keep me from falling and to present me faultless before the presence of *His* glory with exceeding joy. To the only wise *God*, my *Saviour*, be glory and majesty, dominion and power, both now and forever.

My parents, William James and Victoria Nichols: the pair of you always cause me to triumph.

My brother, Raymond, and my sister, Theresa: I win because the two of you live.

My sister-in-law, Alesia Nichols. We're tight like glue.

Joylynn Jossel, an editor extraordinaire you are. Thank you, thank you, thank you for pushing, pulling and stretching me. There was a time when the contractions were unbearable. I wanted to quit but you labored and toiled with me. You held my hand tightly and taught me how to breathe as I pushed this baby out. Your expertise is greatly appreciated.

Ella Curry, the best publicist on this side of heaven. You found the world for me. What would I do without you?

Yolunda Rena McCann, I still remember the day my phone rang. It was you saying, "Let's go to church."

Miss Daphne Smith, my biggest and most devoted fan.

Rico, there are no words, but you know what's in my heart.

Chapter 1

Amaryllis stood across the street from the Holy Deliverance Baptist Church watching the festivities. Thirty feet away from her, Randall, dressed in a white tuxedo, stood next to a white stretch Hummer limousine that was waiting to drive him, his wife and three children off into the sunset. Amaryllis choked back tears as she fought so hard not to swallow. Her left eye, blackened and almost swollen shut, made it difficult for her to witness the celebration and get a good look at Randall's bride. It wasn't until Gabrielle turned in her direction to receive hugs and kisses from family and church members that Amaryllis was allowed to see the face of the woman who had taken her place in Randall's life.

She scanned Gabrielle's face and body, looking for something that would attract Randall to her. Gabrielle wasn't a diva in Amaryllis' eyes. Gabrielle didn't have highlights in her hair, and the only make-up she wore, as far as Amaryllis could tell from where she stood, was a soft layer of burgundy lip gloss. When Gabrielle let go of the embrace she was in, Amaryllis saw the crucifix around her neck sparkle. She knew right then that although Gabrielle wasn't a drop-dead gorgeous beauty, she had the one thing that Amaryllis didn't have-a heart for God, and more than anything, that was what Randall really desired in a woman.

Amaryllis shifted her weight to ease the pressure from her broken leg. She repositioned the crutches and leaned her body against one. Randall looked happy. At least, from across the street he did. She saw his son, Joshua, wrap his arms around Randall's legs and hold on for dear life. Randall seemed to enjoy having this boy in his life. Amaryllis watched as Randall knelt to whisper words in Joshua's ear and give him an encouraging pat on his shoulder. Joshua nodded in understanding of what his father whispered to him, yet, he still hung onto Randall for a sense of security. It was almost as if Joshua thought someone would snatch him away from Randall if he loosened his grip.

In the cradle of his right arm, Randall held his youngest daughter, Eboni. She lay comfortably on his shoulder, facing away from all the well-wishers who tried to pinch her cheek. The look on Eboni's face told the world that she didn't want to be bothered, and if Daddy tried to get her to say 'hello' one more time, she was gonna scream.

The small, petite fingers joined with Randall's right hand belonged to his eldest daughter, Tamika. Amaryllis could tell she was definitely a Daddy's girl. She was friendlier than her sister. Tamika stood proudly next to Randall in her miniature wedding gown, swinging her little flower basket back and forth, watching everyone make a fuss over Uncle Cordell's and Daddy's double wedding. The pastor and his best friend, marrying identical twin sisters, had been the hot topic of the church for weeks.

Someone spoke to Eboni and she swiftly turned her face away and buried her nose in the crook of Randall's neck, trying to get away from the crowd and drown out the noise. That's when Amaryllis saw Randall and his family get into the Hummer. Apparently Eboni had had enough excitement for one day, and Randall seemed to want to get her to a more relaxed atmosphere.

Amaryllis saw Randall and Cordell embrace before Randall got inside of the limousine and it pulled away from the curb. She stood watching the back of the limousine until it disappeared from her sight.

"Amaryllis?" Cordell was standing on the curb with his arm wrapped around his wife's waist when he called out to her.

Amaryllis hadn't wanted either Randall or Cordell to see her, and now it was too late to get out of view. She blamed Cordell for the failure of her and Randall's relationship. From the very beginning, he was against it and voiced his opinion to Randall every chance he got. Today, if Amaryllis didn't know any better, she'd swear Cordell wore a sneer on his face that said, "How you like us now?" She stuck her middle finger up at Cordell then turned and limped down the street on her crutches.

The beating she had received from Darryl was taking its toll on her body. One morning, a month before Randall's wedding, Amaryllis had called Bridgette, her best friend and co-worker, at the law office, saying she'd be a few hours late getting to work. She had become accustomed to spending more and more time in between Darryl's sheets, as long as he was paying for her company.

Darryl had called Amaryllis up that morning, saying he'd make it worth her while if she joined him for an early morning rendezvous. For the love of money and the riverboat casino where she indulged her gambling habit, Amaryllis would do almost anything. She had been living with her mother, Veronica, since her break-up with Randall.

Veronica had walked past Amaryllis' bedroom and saw her packing massage oil in a duffel bag. "Why are you taking that stuff to work?"

Amaryllis zipped the bag closed. "I'm going in late today. Darryl called."

Veronica was pleased. "I see that I taught you well. When the opportunity to make money knocks, you're supposed to open the door. Make that money, honey, and don't forget to give me my cut. If it wasn't for my genes that made you as pretty as you are, men wouldn't give you a second look."

Amaryllis admired herself in the mirror. "Mirror mirror on the wall, who's the finest one of all?"

Veronica stepped behind her daughter and looked at her reflection. "Amaryllis Price is. Now go on and get out of here; duty calls. And remember what I taught you. Closed legs don't get fed."

While she drove north on Interstate 294, Amaryllis was on an emotional high. Darryl had told her he'd make it worth her while, and considering the fact that she would miss at least two hours of work. Having to pay Bridgette to cover her workload until she got to the office would cost Darryl big time.

Amaryllis was grateful for Bridgette. Had it not been for her friendship, Amaryllis, an administrative assistant, couldn't have gotten away with half of the things she did. But Bridgette wasn't a cheap friend. Amaryllis had paid a high price each time she played hooky from work. She didn't mind though. As long as Darryl's posse kept selling drugs for him, he was happy. And the happier Darryl was, the more generous he was with his money. As she drove, she wondered what types of kinky things Darryl would want her to partake in. When she got to his house, she would tell Darryl her price had gone up. Since he'd said that he would make it worth her while, Amaryllis would hold him to it.

She drove through the black iron gates that led her into the familiar community of estate homes and mini-mansions in Long Grove, Illinois. She parked her car in the circular driveway behind Darryl's Escalade. Amaryllis saw a baby blue, late model Dodge Charger and a candy apple red Ford Mustang parked outside the four-car garage. On the telephone, Darryl had given Amaryllis the impression they'd be alone.

She opened the unlocked door and entered the foyer. Darryl yelled from the master suite for her to come upstairs. When Amaryllis walked through the open double doors to the master suite, she saw Darryl lying in the middle of his California king sized bed completely naked. Obviously, foreplay wouldn't be necessary. Darryl was ready.

"Looks like you've started without me," she said.

"Nah, I'm just laying here waiting in anticipation."

Amaryllis glanced outside the master suite door, looking to see if anyone else was in the house with her and Darryl. "I saw two cars outside. Who else is here?"

Darryl shrugged his shoulders. "Just three friends who stayed over."

Amaryllis undressed and got into bed with Darryl, all prepared to give him a massage with the body oil she'd brought.

"Uh, baby, I thought we'd try something different this time," Darryl said.

"If you want something other than the usual, it's gonna cost you."

Darryl ran a soft hand over Amaryllis's bare back. "You know money is no object. How freaky are you?"

Amaryllis's eyebrows raised a bit. She wasn't prepared for this question. "What do you mean?"

"How far are you willing to go?"

It was all about the money with Amaryllis. "How much do you wanna spend?"

From beneath his pillow, Darryl presented Amaryllis with a wad of one hundred dollar bills folded in a brass money clip. She removed the clip and counted ten thousand dollars and smiled wickedly. "For this, I can be as freaky as you want me to be."

Darryl laid back on the bed and positioned his arms behind his head. Just as Amaryllis started to get her groove on with him, she felt a hand, not belonging to Darryl, caress her right shoulder. Amaryllis turned to see three naked men standing next to the bed. She immediately recognized their faces and recalled dancing for them and other professional athletes at a bachelor party at Darryl's house a year and a half ago. The man standing the closest to the bed, Amaryllis remembered as the groom. She saw the platinum wedding band as he pleasured himself. Amaryllis hopped off of Darryl to cover herself with the silk sheets. Her face held a horrifying expression.

"What the heck is going on?" she asked.

"You said you could be as freaky as I wanted you to be," Darryl said to her.

"Yeah, as *you* wanted me to be, Darryl, not them." As she responded to Darryl, Amaryllis eyed the other men in disgust.

Darryl firmly gripped her arm. "They each paid a high price for you."

Whatever Darryl had planned for Amaryllis to do with these men was not happening. She tried to wiggle her wrist free of his tight grip. "I don't care, Darryl. I'm not down with this and you're hurting my arm."

He yanked Amaryllis' arm and threw her onto the bed.

"Do not embarrass me in front of my people. You're gonna give them their money's worth."

Amaryllis tried to escape, but the groom caught her and threw her back on the bed.

Darryl slapped her face. "Didn't I tell you not to embarrass me?"

When Amaryllis began kicking, screaming, and hollering, Darryl punched her jaw with a blow that took her breath away. He instructed the groom to hold her arms, and the other two men to grab her legs and spread them wide. Amaryllis lay on the bed like a rag doll as Darryl gave the groom permission to have his way with her. The more Amaryllis screamed, the harder Darryl's punches became. She tried her best to fight and wiggle free from their grips. Darryl flipped Amaryllis over while one man held her arms down and she felt her shoulder snap out of place.

She screamed again and Darryl punched her in her left eye. "Shut up and be still," he ordered.

The pain and torture was too much for Amaryllis to bare. She managed to free her legs and cross them. Two men grabbed one leg each and forcefully separated them so far apart, she felt as if they had broken her pelvis. Amaryllis screamed and cried as the men, including Darryl, mauled her broken body.

After what seemed like an eternity, the men released Amaryllis's arms and legs. All but Darryl left the master suite. He wasn't phased at her bruised torso and tear stained face. He threw the money she had earned on the bed. "Get up and get out of my house."

Amaryllis winced and moaned at every move she made. She could only work with one arm and one leg. She got dressed as fast and as best as she could, and when she carefully made her way down the spiral staircase, with the cash in her hand, she saw the men sitting in the living room drinking and smoking.

Darryl stood and came to her as she tried to hurry out the front door. He gripped the back of Amaryllis' neck and turned her face toward his own. "What happened to you, Amaryllis?"

She looked into his eyes as tears streamed from her own. She knew what her answer had to be. "I slipped and fell down the stairs."

Darryl released her neck and softly kissed her tears. "Good girl. Go and get yourself checked out."

Amaryllis drove onto Interstate 294 heading south, moaning and crying. She sat lopsided because of her painful, injured pelvis, and her shoulder felt like knives were piercing her. Her vision began to fade and then she saw nothing. Amaryllis' silver Nissan Maxima veered right into a ditch at sixty miles per hour.

Amaryllis woke up five hours later in the intensive care unit at Illinois Masonic Hospital. When she was questioned about her injuries, Amaryllis stated that she had fallen down a flight of stairs at a friend's house and was driving herself to the emergency room when she lost consciousness.

Veronica sat quietly by Amaryllis' side as she told her story. When they were finally alone, she looked at her daughter. "Amaryllis, what really happened at Darryl's house?"

Stitches sewn in the corners of her mouth made it difficult for Amaryllis to speak. "He wanted to share me with three other men."

"Were they paying?" Veronica asked without warmth or compassion for her daughter's injuries.

Amaryllis's left eye was covered with bandages. With her right eye, she frowned at her mother. "What difference does it make, Veronica? I wasn't gonna let them use me like that."

As usual, Veronica only focused on money. "So, you got your butt whipped for free? You ain't got nothin' to show for your bruises?"

"I got my money."

Veronica stood from the chair she was seated in, looking around the hospital room for Amaryllis' purse. "Well, can I have my cut so I can go?"

"I can't believe you're looking at me lying here half dead and asking me for money that you did nothing for."

"Half dead means half alive. You're gonna be all right."

Amaryllis pointed toward the closet where her personal items had been stored. "Veronica, take your cut out of my purse and get out of here."

Veronica counted out five thousand dollars and placed the money in her bra. She kissed her daughter's forehead and left the hospital room. "Good job, baby. You made Momma real proud."

For two weeks after the assault, Amaryllis attended physical therapy daily to get her pelvis and shoulder in working order. She hadn't seen or heard from Veronica since she'd come to get her cut of the money. Amaryllis had taken a leave of absence from work and moved in with Bridgette. It was a week later when she'd seen the article in the *Chicago Sun-Times* that was entitled:

Cordell Bryson, Pastor of Holy Deliverance Baptist Church, And Best Friend, Randall Loomis, To Wed Identical Twins Tomorrow.

And now, here she was, watching as Randall's limousine vanished from her sight. After giving Cordell the finger, Amaryllis went back to Bridgette's apartment to call her sister, Michelle, in Las Vegas, Nevada. Amaryllis felt that she needed a fresh start in a new city. She hoped Michelle would help her out.

"Hi, Michelle, it's Amaryllis," she said into the phone receiver.

Michelle Denise Price, Amaryllis' elder by two years, was always happy to hear her younger sister's voice. The girls' father, Nicholas Price, had met and married Amaryllis' mother, Veronica, after Michelle's mother died. But after a year of arguing and fighting over money issues, Nicholas decided he'd be much happier without the stress Veronica poured into their marriage. He filed for divorce, packed up two-and-a-half-year-old Michelle and headed for Las Vegas, Nevada. Six months later, Nicholas received a call from Veronica informing him that his daughter, named Amaryllis, had been born.

Having grown up separately, Michelle with their father and Amaryllis with her mother, the two sisters, through telephone calls and summer visits, managed to become close and remain close though they lived thousands of miles apart.

"Hey there, long time no hear. How's my baby sister doing? What have you been up to?" Michelle asked.

Amaryllis exhaled. "A whole lot. I was wondering if I could come and stay with you for a while."

Michelle stood and waited anxiously for her sister at the security gate. Amaryllis came through the terminal of the McCarran International Airport looking beaten down and broken up. Her left eye was still swollen and dark. The stitches in the corners of her lips were very visible. She limped on a cane and a cast supported her right arm. Michelle didn't recognize her sister. She made eye contact with Amaryllis then looked past her.

Amaryllis came and stood next to Michelle. "Do I look that bad that my own sister doesn't recognize me?"

Michelle looked into the face of someone she once knew as beautiful and well put together. It wasn't often that she got to see Amaryllis, but when she did, Amaryllis always had her hair, nails and make up done to perfection. Michelle wore a horrid expression. She was shocked at how grotesque Amaryllis' face looked. "Oh my God; what happened to you? Were you in some kind of accident?"

"Yeah, I accidentally walked into a fist."

Michelle reached out to hug her, but Amaryllis cautiously stepped backward. Three weeks had passed since Amaryllis' unfortunate encounter with Darryl and his posse, but her body was still very sore. "No, please don't touch me; it hurts too much."

"Oh, Amaryllis, how could you let something like this happen?"

"Do you have forever and a day for me to tell you about it? That's how long it'll take me."

Michelle relieved Amaryllis' left arm of her carry on tote. "First, let's get your luggage, then I'll take you home and get you into a nice comfy bed. I told Daddy that you were coming and he's excited."

It was no secret to Amaryllis that their father favored Michelle. "Yeah, I bet. Why is he so excited to see his daughter whom he's always called *The Bad Seed*?"

"Don't go there, Amaryllis. Growing up, you were a brat and you know it. How many Catholic school girls do you know get arrested at eight years old for pushing a nun down the steps?"

"Well, the heifer shouldn't have taken my candy. She didn't buy it."

"It was still wrong for you to do that."

"Okay, so I do one bad thing as a child and folks never let me forget it."

They had been slowly walking to the baggage claim area when Michelle abruptly stopped walking and looked at Amaryllis. "Excuse *me? One* bad thing? Let's take a walk down memory lane, shall we? You gave Daddy hell every time you came to visit. How about that time when we were at summer camp and you put hair remover in Karla Monroe's shampoo? It took almost three years for that girl's hair to grow back."

"Well, she shouldn't have called me fatso."

"That's beside the point, Amaryllis. Karla calling you names didn't hurt you, but what *you* did tormented her for years."

"Okay, so I did two bad things," Amaryllis said as they resumed walking.

"*Two* bad things, Amaryllis? I don't think so. Remember the summer when you came to visit when you sat and waited for our neighbor, Mrs. Taylor, to leave at night to go to work? Every night you watched her husband's girlfriend sneak in the back door. You decided to take pictures of her going in the house for a week then mail the pictures anonymously to Mrs. Taylor."

"Come on now, Michelle, you know good and well that he was wrong for cheating on his wife."

"It was none of your business."

"He stopped cheating didn't he?"

"He had no choice after Mrs. Taylor hired two goons to break both of his legs."

"Mrs. Taylor didn't seem to mind pushing him around the neighborhood in a wheelchair."

Michelle chuckled. "Of course not. With two broken legs, she didn't have to worry about him creepin' anymore."

"Okay, Michelle; I did three bad things."

Michelle stopped walking again and looked at Amaryllis. "*Three* bad things? What about that time when you—"

"Hey, I didn't come all this way to walk down memory lane with you."

"You're the one who seemed to have forgotten why your nickname is *The Bad Seed*."

"Well, thanks to you, now I remember. Can we please get out of this airport? My leg is killing me and it's hot as heck here in Vegas."

Michelle grabbed Amaryllis softly around her waist and carefully led her to the baggage claim area. "We only got a little ways to go. Lean on me. And as far as the weather goes, September in Vegas is like July in Chicago."

At twenty-eight years old, Michelle was the youngest and only African American female attorney who owned and ran a law firm in the entire city of Reno. Price & Associates sat in the heart of the city. It housed six female attorneys who were all working for Michelle. It wasn't that she discriminated against men, but the women who came to her, fresh out of law school, expressed how difficult it was to get hired in the law business. Michelle could relate to their frustrations because she, too, was interviewed and hired by a female partner after being turned away many times by other firms due to her gender.

Two months at the law firm, Michelle was made partner, and in only three years, she managed to save enough money to invest in a building of her own. She vowed to herself that she would give as many women as she could a chance in life. Corporate law was her expertise and her skills blew the minds of business owners who challenged Michelle and her team in the courtroom. Michelle's all-female staff was fierce.

Price & Associates had been in business for two and a half years and had never lost a case. In the past eight months it had gone from being the ninth best law firm out of seventeen in the city, to the third best. Michelle was confident in herself and her team to know that in another year, they'd be ranked the best and most requested corporate law firm in Reno, Nevada.

Michelle owned a three-level town home on North Bally Street, located on the east side of Las Vegas. Though she lived alone, the town home consisted of four bedrooms, one of which housed her home office, a laundry room and a full bath, all on the third floor. The entire second floor dedicated itself to Michelle's master suite and bath. This room surrounded her king-sized white wicker bed, nightstand, eight-drawer dresser, full-length mirror and bench that was placed at the foot of her bed. This room also held a compact refrigerator, a thirty-two inch flat screen television and a cherry stained marble fireplace.

Toward the front of the master bedroom, Michelle designed a sitting room with two chaise chairs, a glass cocktail table and a five-shelf bookcase that held a collection of novels written by African-American authors. This is where Michelle spent her time when she wasn't in the courtroom. She would curl up on one of the chaise chairs and read away the hours. Christian fiction novels were her favorite books to read. Michelle took pride in her book collection.

On the cocktail table, sat her latest delivery from Black Expressions Book Club. Michelle did so much reading that she vowed to take at least six months off from practicing law in the near future and write her own novel. Surely she could find something to write about. How she made it to the top as a young black attorney would be a great start.

On the first floor of the town home were the kitchen,

dining and living rooms. A half bath was just off the kitchen and a door adjacent to the bath led to the two and a half car garage where Michelle stored her Lincoln Navigator and late model Jaguar X-Type.

Amaryllis loved the town home and was in awe of its décor and magnitude. As Michelle escorted her from room to room, Amaryllis could actually see herself in a home of her own. When Michelle opened the door to the garage, Amaryllis froze.

Michelle saw the look on Amaryllis' face. "What's wrong?" Amaryllis couldn't take her eyes away from the Jaguar. Michelle followed her gaze to the car and asked her again. "Amaryllis, what's wrong?"

Still unable to move or respond, Amaryllis kept her focus on the car. Michelle slowly walked and stood in front of her and saw tears on the verge of falling onto her cheeks. Amaryllis blinked and the teardrops fell onto her face.

Michelle wiped the tears away. "Honey, I can't help if you don't tell me what's wrong."

Amaryllis forced herself to look away from the car and into her sister's eyes. "You remember the guy I told you about; the one I lived with a year ago?"

"Yeah, his name was Randall, right?"

"He had a Jaguar exactly like yours."

Michelle didn't see the connection between Amaryllis' tears and Randall's car. "Why is that upsetting you?"

Amaryllis wiped her tears away. "Because I'm reminded of Black."

Michelle frowned. "Who?"

"Black."

"Who is Black?"

"Randall is Black."

"I know he's a black man."

"No, his name is Black."

"Randall Black?," Michelle asked.

"No, Black *is* Randall."

Michelle shrugged her shoulders. "Amaryllis, you're not making any sense."

"Black is the nickname I gave Randall because he's so dark."

"Oh, I see. Thanks for clearing that up. But why the tears about the car?"

"Looking at the Jaguar reminds me of the good times Black and I had. We went everywhere in his Jaguar before . . ." She got choked up and couldn't finish her sentence.

Michelle wiped away the new tears that made their appearance. "Before what, honey?"

"Before I asked Darryl to get his boys to trash it." Amaryllis couldn't hold the cry any longer. She shifted her weight, leaned on the door to the garage, put her face in her hands and let it all out. "Oh, Michelle, I've destroyed the best thing that has ever happened to me."

Michelle reached out to her sister and held her tight. "Shh, it's all right, sweetie. Come on and let's get you off of this leg."

Amaryllis chose the largest guest bedroom on the third floor. Michelle helped her undress and get into bed. She fluffed the pillows for Amaryllis then brewed chamomile tea and brought her a cup. "This should calm your nerves a bit. Are you hungry?"

Amaryllis took a sip of the tea, leaned back on the pillows, exhaled and closed her eyes. "I don't have much of an appetite, but my shoulder is starting to ache. Can you get my pills? They're in my purse on the dresser."

Michelle gave Amaryllis two pills then filled a cup with tap water from the bathroom faucet.

"What is this you're taking?" she asked Amaryllis.

"It's Vicodin. I love this stuff because it numbs my whole body."

"Well, maybe you shouldn't drink the chamomile tea right now." Michelle knew the effects of chamomile. Whenever she needed to wind down after a difficult day in the courtroom, the chamomile tea acted as a lullaby. She worried what the tea mixed with the Vicodin may do to Amaryllis.

"I want to drink it. I need all the relaxation I can get."

Michelle sat at the foot of the bed and watched Amaryllis drink the tea. "Can I ask you a question?"

"You can ask, but I can't guarantee a complete answer before the Vicodin kicks in."

"I'm curious about Darryl. Who was he and why did you ask him to trash Randall's car?"

Amaryllis set the empty teacup on the nightstand and positioned herself to lie comfortably on the bed. "Darryl is the man who's got me looking the way I do. Back when I thought he was a nice guy, I asked him to do this favor for me because I was angry at Randall for cuttin' off my gambling money."

"I thought you gave up gambling years ago. How much did this favor cost you?"

"I paid with my body," Amaryllis admitted shamefully.

Michelle blinked her eyes repeatedly. "You what?"

"You heard me," Amaryllis said, feeling embarrassed by her past actions.

Michelle couldn't imagine her sister doing such a thing. "You sacrificed your body, Amaryllis?"

"I'm not proud of it. Money became tight when Black got suspended from his job. Darryl was there financially to pick up where he left off."

"How long were you sleeping with Darryl?"

"Long enough for him to rape and beat me up."

"Is he the reason you and Randall broke up?"

"I guess you can say that. Black followed me to Darryl's house one night and saw me stripping for him and his friends. When I got home that night, Black told me to get out of his house. He hasn't spoken to me since. Now he's married with three kids and living in a mansion in Oakbrook, Illinois. I'm supposed to be living in that house, Michelle. Those are supposed to be my kids. Black shared his dreams with me and I practically laughed in his face. And look at me now."

Amaryllis started crying again and Michelle patted her foot. "Honey, we all go through rough times. Nothing just happens. There's something good coming out of your experience. The most important thing is that you learn from your mistakes and not repeat them. The next good man that comes in your life will be appreciated, right?"

When Amaryllis didn't respond, Michelle looked at her and saw that she was softly snoring. Michelle was glad her sister was in town. She hoped that this visit would be good for their father and Amaryllis to bridge the gap between them.

Michelle and their father, Nicholas, lived a saved life. Amaryllis was the complete opposite. She didn't care about church or God. Michelle realized her sister's soul was at stake and she vowed to do all she could to help Amaryllis develop a heart for God.

Chapter 2

Later on in the evening, as Amaryllis slept, Michelle decided to return to the firm to finish paperwork she had put aside when she left to meet Amaryllis at the airport. She was in the middle of looking over a brief when she glanced at the eight-by-ten photograph of her fiancé.

Minister James Bradley was heaven sent and Michelle knew it. God confirmed that revelation shortly after Michelle set her eyes on him for the first time. James had swept Michelle off of her feet the moment he spoke to her.

Michelle picked up the silver-plated frame that embraced the photo of the man that would soon be her husband. Looking at James' smile, the corners of Michelle's own lips curled upward. There wasn't a stress filled day when his dimples hadn't come to her rescue. She kissed James' picture as she reminisced about the day God answered her prayer one year ago. It all happened on a Sunday night at the Praise Temple Church of God. Michelle had stood in the vestibule after the radio broadcast, talking to her best friend, Jodie Frazier, when out of nowhere, a perfect gentleman approached her. He gently applied his opened palm against Michelle's lower back, interrupting her in mid-sentence.

"Excuse me, I've been watching you for weeks and trying to get up the nerve to approach you. I'm drawn to your spirit and level of praise. Your true worship shows that you're a woman after God's own heart and I like that. And if no one has ever told you before, let me be the first to say that you are one beautiful black woman."

This stranger's words had literally knocked Michelle off of her feet. She had only been a member of Praise Temple Church of God for a few months and hadn't become acquainted with many of the members. She certainly didn't know the Adonis standing in front of her. Dark brown eyes, skin the color of burnt butterscotch, a freshly groomed goatee blended with a mustache that cascaded upward to side burns stood in Michelle's presence. She almost lost her balance when she inhaled his cologne, Tiffany's Man. Michelle recognized the scent. Last Christmas she'd bought a bottle for seventy-five dollars an ounce for her father.

The words that flowed from this gentleman's lips had never been spoken to Michelle before. "Thank you," she smiled.

He smiled in return. "What's your name?"

Michelle saw deep dimples in each cheek and the whitest teeth she'd ever seen. His mother must've slapped braces on him at age five. Michelle immediately fell head over heels in love with a man whose name she didn't know. When she realized his hand was still in place on her back she felt her body temperature rise fifty degrees. "Michelle Denise Price."

His smile got wider. No doubt, he was expecting only a first name, but she had given him three. "I'm Minister

James Bradley. It is certainly a pleasure to make your acquaintance, Michelle Denise Price."

James greeted Jodie, gave Michelle one last smile and walked away. Michelle's eyes followed James as he entered the pastor's office and closed the door behind him.

"Jodie, who was that angel?"

"James is Bishop Graham's armor bearer. Whenever and wherever you see the Bishop, you see James. You've never noticed him before?"

"No. Is he dating anyone?"

"Not that I know of. James' duties as an armor bearer have him so busy that no one can get close to him."

"Well, I'm gonna have to do something about that."

"I see stars in your eyes, Michelle. But you won't get to James. He appears with Bishop Graham and disappears with him."

"Oh, I'll get to James," Michelle said with confidence.

Driving home from church, Michelle couldn't get James Bradley out of her mind. She muted the radio and talked to God. "What just happened back there, Lord? Is James the husband I've been praying for?"

She reminisced what James had said to her only moments earlier. *"I'm drawn to your spirit and level of praise. You're a woman after God's own heart and I like that. And you are one beautiful black woman."*

Michelle couldn't contain herself. She smiled at the recall of James' words. "Oh God, can I *please* have him?"

MY DAUGHTER, I'VE JUST DEALT YOU A PROMISING HAND. IT'S UP TO YOU TO PLAY YOUR CARDS RIGHT.

The following Sunday morning, James was disappointed that he didn't see Michelle at morning service. He had no clue where she was, but had a good idea who may know

Michelle's whereabouts. After the benediction, he sought out Jodie, who was making her way downstairs to the fellowship hall. "Praise the Lord, Sister Frazier."

"Praise the Lord, Minister Bradley, how are you?" Jodie smiled.

"I'm fine, thank you. And how are *you*?"

"Sleep deprived," Jodie chuckled.

"I can understand why. I just ran into your husband, Michael. He tells me that little Mya is quite active during the night hours."

"Hmph, like he'd know with all the noise he makes, sawing logs."

James laughed. "Listen, I was wondering if you know where your friend, Michelle, is."

Jodie returned James' smile. "Michelle decided to go to work today."

"I see. What kind of work does she do?"

"She owns a law firm."

His eyebrows shot up in the air. "Is that so?"

"Yes, Price & Associates. It's on Vegas Drive downtown."

The wheels in James' head were turning. "Price & Associates on Vegas Drive. Okay, thanks a lot, Sister Frazier."

James turned to walk away and Jodie called after him. "Shall I tell Michelle you asked about her?"

"If you like," he smiled.

Monday morning just before noon, Michelle sat behind her desk looking over briefs when her telephone extension rang.

"Guess who asked your whereabouts in church yesterday?" Jodie said.

"Minister Bradley?" Michelle was hopeful.

"Yes. Apparently he's into you just as much as you are into him."

"That's good to know, Jodie. He has the most gorgeous smile I've ever seen."

"I can't deny that. Hey, let's meet for lunch."

Michelle looked at the amount of paperwork on her desk and exhaled. "Sorry, I can't. I'm preparing for a major trial next week. I've got tons of paperwork to—" Michelle abruptly stopped talking. Her eyes were fixed on the masculine figure standing in her doorway. James Bradley was present with a dozen roses in one hand, a picnic basket in the other, and that famous gorgeous smile on his face.

Jodie was still waiting on the other end of the telephone for Michelle to complete her sentence. "Hello? Michelle, are you there?"

Michelle couldn't move. James walked over to her, set the picnic basket on top of her desk, gently took the telephone from her hand and spoke into the receiver. "This is James Bradley. I'm sorry that Miss Price can't continue this conversation due to the fact that she's about to be swept off her feet. She will be out of the office for the remainder of the day."

Thinking back on that time caused Michelle's heart to go pitter-patter. She let out a loud sigh, kissed James' picture again, and placed it back on her desk. It was getting late and she still had to look over two more briefs before she went home to check on Amaryllis. Michelle was also excited that Amaryllis would finally meet her prince. Amaryllis' past relationships with men were nothing to write home about. Michelle hoped that while she was visiting, Amaryllis would take notes and learn from her and James how a relationship between a man and a woman should be played out.

Chapter 3

Around eight o'clock P.M., the ringing of the telephone aroused Amaryllis from a comatose-like sleep. She reached for the telephone on her nightstand and answered, sounding very groggy.

"Hi, beautiful. Did I wake you?" a man's voice asked.

Feeling the effects of the Vicodin and chamomile tea, Amaryllis was delirious and had no clue where she was or who the man was she was talking to. "Uh-huh."

"Why are you in bed so early. Did you have a bad day?"

"Uh-huh."

"Is there anything I can do to make you feel better?"

"Uh-huh."

"How about I go to your favorite Chinese restaurant and get some of that Mongolian Beef you like so much, then swing by your place? Would you like that?"

"Uh-huh." In the faint distance of her mind, Amaryllis heard the line go dead and she released the telephone from her hand.

* * *

At 9:15 P.M., James Bradley was standing outside of Michelle's town home ringing the doorbell without getting an answer. Using his cellular telephone, he called her home number and got a busy signal. James rang the doorbell again. Still no answer. He decided to call Michelle's cellular number. He knew that no matter what Michelle was doing, she always answered her cellular phone in case it was a business call. She was sitting behind her desk at the law firm when she answered his call.

"Hello, handsome."

"Mickey, why won't you let me in?" James always chose to use his nickname for Michelle.

"What do you mean?"

"I'm standing outside; can't you hear the doorbell?"

"It must be out of order. Hang on and I'll buzz you in."

"A buzzer? That's just pure laziness, Mickey."

Michelle's office was on the sixth floor. Of course, she'd buzz him. "James, I know I need to exercise, but if you think that I'm getting ready to walk down six flights of stairs to open the door, you've got another thing coming."

"You only have three floors, Mickey. Have you been drinking?"

"No, I haven't and I'm buzzing the door. Are you in yet?"

"I can't hear the buzzer; it must be out of order too. We wouldn't have to go through this if you gave me a key to your house."

"That's out of the question, James, and how would a key to my house benefit you if you're trying to get into my office?"

"Your office?" James frowned.

"Yes; that's where I am."

"What are you talking about, Mickey? Why would you go to your office when you knew I was bringing dinner to your house?"

"I *didn't* know. You should've called."

James exhaled but kept his cool. "Mickey, did I not talk to you an hour ago and say that I was bringing Chinese food to your place?"

"No, James, you didn't. You must've called one of your other women, because you certainly didn't talk to me," Michelle joked.

James stood outside the town home dumbfounded. "Don't go there, Mickey. You know good and well there are no other women. Why are you playing with me?"

"Honestly, James, I don't remember you calling me here."

"I didn't call your office; I called your house."

A light bulb went on in Michelle's head. "Oh, my goodness. You must've talked to Amaryllis."

"Who?"

"My sister, Amaryllis. Remember I told you she was coming to stay with me for a while."

"That explains it then. I thought you were out of it from having a bad day."

"She's on heavy pain medication, but if she can't hear the doorbell, I wonder if it's too heavy."

"You want me to bring dinner to the law office?"

"No, sweetie, stay put. I'll be there in ten minutes."

Michelle pushed aside the brief she was reading and turned off her desk lamp. She left the law office in a hurry, excited to see her man. As she drove into her driveway, she saw James sitting on the steps. She got out of the car and walked over to him. "Hello, gorgeous," she greeted with a wide grin.

James looked at her with his prize-winning smile that always melted Michelle. With his deep dimples in both cheeks, sometimes Michelle had to turn her head to break the stare. But James had the kind of smile that drew a person to him. He had all the qualities that a woman could want in a man. He was gentle, extremely handsome, kind, warmhearted, generous, loving, and most importantly, he was saved and sanctified. But out of all these qualities, it was his smile that most attracted Michelle to him.

James stood and kissed her lightly on the lips, then reached for her hand to help her up the steps. "You're the gorgeous one, Mickey."

"Uh-uh. You are."

"No, you are."

Each and every time James and Michelle came together, this was the greeting they shared. If there was ever a time when one of them didn't compliment the other on who was the more gorgeous of the two, something was wrong.

Michelle entered the town home and James followed. "Mickey, I'm gonna get dinner set on the table. Are you hungry?" James asked as he headed toward the kitchen.

"I'm famished, but I gotta check on my sister first. She's been asleep way too long."

"Didn't you say she's on heavy medication?"

"But I also gave her chamomile tea. You go ahead and start without me."

Michelle climbed the stairs to the third floor. She walked into Amaryllis' room and turned on the light. Next to the bed, Michelle saw the telephone on the floor. Amaryllis was lying on her stomach with her hair strewn about her face. Michelle placed the telephone on its base, then sat down on the bed and tapped Amaryllis's shoulder.

"Amaryllis, sweetie, wake up."

Amaryllis stirred, but made no effort to turn over. Michelle removed her hair from her face and shook her. Amaryllis mumbled something, but didn't move. Michelle stood and pulled the sheets from her. She rolled Amaryllis onto her back and lightly tapped her face. "Amaryllis, please wake up; you're scaring me."

She sleepily opened one eye. "Why are you bothering me, Michelle?"

"Because you've been asleep since this morning."

"And?"

"And it's almost nine-thirty at night."

"And?"

"And you need to get up and eat something."

Amaryllis rolled onto her stomach. "I'm not hungry, I'm sleepy."

"We've got to get you off of that Vicodin. Somebody could've broken in here and taken everything and you would've never known it."

Amaryllis quickly sat up. "Girl, if you touch my Vicodin, I'll put a serious hurting on you."

"Yeah, whatever. James is downstairs and he bought Chinese food. I want you to meet him, so let's get you washed up and dressed so you can come down and eat with us."

"Michelle, I look a mess and I don't want him to meet me for the first time with me looking all bruised up. What will he think?"

"He won't think anything; James doesn't know what happened to you."

"I'm not going downstairs," Amaryllis protested.

"You have to eat."

"So, I'll eat up here, in my room."

"Amaryllis, James is here at least twice a week. He's bound to run into you sooner or later."

"Let it be later then."

Michelle helped Amaryllis into the bathroom and started the water in the shower. When she saw Amaryllis struggling with her broken shoulder to get undressed, she assisted her. She helped Amaryllis into the tub and gave her a bar of soap and a wash towel. "Are you gonna be okay by yourself?"

"Yeah, I'll be fine."

"I'll come back up in ten minutes to check on you." Michelle left the bathroom and went to the dresser drawer to lay out a clean pair of underwear and a nightgown on the bed for Amaryllis. Michelle had unpacked her sister's things and placed them in drawers last night, after Amaryllis had passed out from the Vicodin and chamomile tea.

Michelle heard moaning. She went back into the bathroom, pulled the shower curtain back and saw tears streaming down Amaryllis' face. "What's wrong, sweetie?"

"My shoulder hurts when I lift my arm."

Michelle stopped the shower and helped Amaryllis out of the tub. After wrapping a huge terry cloth towel around her, Michelle inserted the plug in the drain, sprinkled a handful of Epsom salt in the tub and ran warm water. After she helped Amaryllis back into the tub and carefully sat her down, Michelle got on her knees, rolled up her sleeves and gently bathed her baby sister. The tears that began streaming down Amaryllis' face concerned Michelle.

"Am I too rough?"

"I feel so helpless, Michelle. And I feel bad because your man is downstairs waiting for you, but you're up here taking care of me."

"James is fine. Trust me; he's got his food and his sports, he's very content."

"I appreciate you accepting me into your home and taking care of me like this."

"You're my sister, girl. It's just me and you, so we gotta take care of each other."

After the bath, Michelle applied lotion to Amaryllis' skin and helped her into her fresh clothing.

"I used to do this for Black. I would bathe him, oil his whole body and cook his meals and then feed him."

Michelle looked at Amaryllis as though she was a nutcase. "You're kidding me, right?"

"No, I took care of Black like that all the time."

"You know that it was wrong for you to do that, don't you?"

"But I enjoyed doing things like that for him."

"And there's nothing wrong with a woman taking care of her man like that as long as he's her husband."

"We lived together, Michelle."

"And that was wrong too. Some things are sacred and should be saved for marriage. If you give a man all the sex he wants, bathe him and cook his every meal, then feed him too, what has he got to look forward to after you say your vows? When you promise to love, honor and cherish your man in the presence of God, that's when the cooking, bathing and sex comes into play. You want to keep a man guessing what else you've got to give, Amaryllis."

"When you're courting your man, he should feel like a kid in a candy store with only a nickel in his pocket. There's so much good stuff that he would like to have a taste of but can't afford. But because he loves candy, it causes him to save his allowance and come back for more when he has enough money. You see, Amaryllis, the candy is there for him to look at and admire, but it's not free. If a man is able to have all the candy he wants without having to pay, sooner or later, he'll lose his appetite for it. Now don't get me wrong; I love James with my whole heart. He's good to me and I'm good to him. But as much as we love each other, he's not worthy of me sexing, bathing and feeding him yet. I give him just enough of me to keep him coming back."

"What do you mean you give him just enough?"

"This is *my* home. I worked very hard to buy this place, and God allowed me to have it. James is not allowed to bring his clothes over and take up space in any of my closets. And even though there are three bathrooms in this house, neither of them has room for James' toothbrush. *I* pay the mortgage, not James. In the entire year that we've been together, he hasn't once spent the night. Even if we're watching a movie that ends at three o'clock in the morning, James has to leave here.

"Another example is the way I cook for him, if I cook at all. I don't like to eat restaurant food all the time, so occasionally, I may cook. I know James' favorite meal is spare ribs, macaroni and cheese, hot water cornbread with mustard and turnip greens. I hooked him up one Sunday after church and the brotha was foaming at the mouth. He said even his mother's greens didn't taste that good. That was about seven months ago and he's been begging for that meal ever since. I tell him that I don't have time to cook it, but I'll try and make it soon. That lets him know that he's got something to look forward to. Now, when I have the time to cook, I do the basic fried chicken or maybe spaghetti, but I don't cook for James everyday. Only my husband will be allowed that luxury. When he becomes my husband, he'll get his greens."

To Amaryllis, Michelle's love life sounded boring. "Okay, Michelle, I get all of that. But to me, it sounds like you and James are just existing. I mean, what do you do for your man? How do you make him feel good?"

Michelle knew what Amaryllis was getting at. "Sex is not a part of our relationship. We hug, kiss and cuddle. However, my body is my most prized possession. James will not receive my goods until we're in covenant with one another."

Amaryllis sat on the edge of her bed and looked at

Michelle in awe. "Are you telling me that you've been dating this man for over a year and he's never touched you?"

"I didn't say James doesn't touch me. He touches me all the time and I touch him, but we're careful *where* we touch each other. I told you that we hug, kiss and cuddle."

Amateurs. "And that's it?"

"That's enough. James and I never put ourselves in a position to be tempted. He's not allowed in my bedroom and I don't enter his. When he's here visiting, I'm dressed appropriately, and when I'm at his house, he's dressed appropriately. We practice discipline and respect. James and I love and honor the Lord too much to be saying 'Please forgive us, we got caught up in the moment'. God forgives, yes. But why put yourself in that place to begin with?"

"When you showed me your bedroom today, I saw lots of pretty lingerie hanging in your closet. Why do you have all of that if you don't wear it?"

"I *do* wear it. But for God, not James."

"Why for God?"

"Because He's my true husband. Some nights, I light scented candles around my Jacuzzi tub, put on praise and worship music, then soak until the water gets cool. I get out and spray on my Perry Ellis or Ralph Lauren perfume, slip into one of those nighties and lie on my bed and tell God how much I love Him. I tell Him that no one can ever do for me what He does for me. Then I let Him know that He's the One that I worship and adore. I let Him know that no man could ever take His place in my life.

"Then I thank Him for my law firm and the home He gave me. I blow kisses at Him and tell Him that not only do I love Him, I'm also *in* love with Him. I assure God that He's my King. When I dress intimately for God, He knows that He's got a part of me that James doesn't. It tells Him that my body is *His* temple, not James'. Then I start to praise God by telling Him how great and wonderful He is to me and how much I appreciate the way He loves me. I let Him know that until He sends my soul mate to me, only He shall have my goods."

Amaryllis sat on the bed and looked at Michelle like she was from another planet. "And you mean to tell me that after doing all of that, you're sexually satisfied?"

"Amaryllis, let me explain something to you. God satisfies me spiritually, mentally, physically and emotionally. When James becomes my husband, he'll be the one to satisfy me in that way."

Amaryllis opted to end Michelle's lesson. All this talk of not sexing a man was giving her a headache. She laid down on the bed with Michelle's help. Once Amaryllis was comfortable, Michelle gave her the television remote.

"I don't know what's on because I rarely watch TV," Michelle said.

"As long as you've got the *Lifetime Movie Network* channel, I'm cool."

"Okay, I'm gonna go down and get your dinner."

"I don't feel like eating anything right now."

"Amaryllis, you've been here since this morning and you haven't eaten a thing. You've gotta put something in your stomach."

"I'm not a Chinese food fan."

"I can make whatever you want."

"Michelle, don't worry about me. You've been up here long enough. Go downstairs and tend to your man."

"After I take care of you, I will. What do you want to eat?"

Amaryllis exhaled loudly to show Michelle she was working on her last nerve. "Nothing."

"Oh, you're gonna eat something, and don't think you'll be chewing on those Vicodin pills all the time." Having said that, Michelle left the bedroom.

Forty-five minutes had passed before Michelle got back downstairs. James had already eaten, washed his plate and was into a football game when Michelle walked past him into the kitchen.

She saw him slouching on the sofa. "Have you eaten yet, sweetie?"

James extended his hands behind his head and stretched. "Yep, now I'm just missing my baby. What's going on up there?"

"I had to help my sister do a few things. I need to make her a bowl of soup. Will you excuse me for another ten minutes?"

"Of course. Isn't she coming down?"

"Not tonight. She's not feeling her best. She's lying down."

"That's too bad; I was looking forward to meeting her."

"Maybe tomorrow when she's feeling better."

Michelle prepared Amaryllis a bowl of chicken noodle soup. She placed the bowl and crackers on a dinner tray next to a glass of apple juice and took it up to Amaryllis. "I've got your favorite soup."

Amaryllis sat up as best she could against the headboard. Michelle placed the dinner tray on her lap. Amaryllis looked at the soup and frowned. "Ugh."

"Don't even try it. You love chicken noodle soup."

"I grew out of it."

"Well, that's too bad, because you're eating it." Michelle sat on the bed and crumbled the crackers in the soup just the way they used to eat it long ago. She stirred the soup and brought a spoonful up to Amaryllis' lips.

"You don't have to feed me, Michelle."

"If I leave it, will you promise to at least eat half of it?"

"I promise that I'll eat a little."

Michelle placed the spoon in the bowl then stood up. "Is there anything else you need?"

"Yes, can you get my Vicodin?"

Michelle got the bottle of pills and went into the bathroom for a cup of water. She poured the Vicodin pills down the sink and filled the empty bottle with regular strength Tylenol from the medicine cabinet. She then brought it and the water to Amaryllis. She watched as Amaryllis swallowed two pills. "Okay, I'm going downstairs to watch the football game with James. If you need anything, just holler."

Amaryllis was astonished. "You actually watch the game with him?"

"Of course." Michelle didn't know why that bit of information would be shocking to Amaryllis.

"But you hate sports."

"I hate watching the game, but I love spending time with my man. And if I have to spend an entire evening yawning from pure boredom, why not benefit from it by lying in his arms?"

"I don't get it."

Michelle shook her head from side to side. "Amaryllis, Amaryllis, Amaryllis, you've got *so* much to learn. It's not about being bored; it's about letting my man know that I care what his interests are. James knows that watching sports is something that I hate with a passion. And he tells me all the time that he doesn't mind me going into another room to watch a different channel or occupying my time doing something else. He's even offered many times to change channels and watch something that I'm interested in. But I know how he is about his sports, so I don't mind recording whatever I wanna see and watching it at a later time.

"If I make James watch the game by himself, then he

might as well have stayed at home. And because he knows that I'm willing to watch a boring game with him despite the fact that I'm not a sports fan, he appreciates me even more. I can't tell you how many times his friends have invited him over to watch a football or basketball game with just the boys. Each time, he declines and comes right over here to watch it with me. The majority of the time, I fall asleep, but James doesn't care because when he looks down, I'm lying right in his arms. I have to let my man know that as long as we're together, I don't care what we do."

"Does he do the same for you?"

"Not really."

"Why not make James watch a movie with you that he thinks is boring, then maybe he'll understand how you feel about sports?"

"Because it's not the same, Amaryllis. Men are different from women. There's no way you'll get a man to watch a movie if he's not interested. It just ain't gonna happen because their attention span won't let it. Men's lives revolve around their women, their cars, their jobs and their sports, not the *Lifetime* channel."

Michelle sat down on the bed. "Let me tell you a story. There was a movie coming on one night that I wanted to see. I told James about it and he agreed to watch it with me. It just so happens that on that same night, there was a championship basketball game on. But James wanted to prove to me that he could sacrifice his games just like I sacrifice my movies. Twenty minutes into the movie, he gets bored. Next thing I know, he's blowing in my ear, trying to suck on my neck and telling me how good I smell. Then he started to unbutton my blouse. That's when I changed the channel to the basketball game.

"Immediately, his attention went toward the television.

So I recorded the rest of my movie, curled up next to James and watched the game. He pulled me into his arms, kissed me and said, 'Thank you, baby.' Sure, he could've spent the evening with his boys yelling at the TV, but he chose to be with me. Do you understand all that I just said, Amaryllis?"

"I guess so. The relationship you have with James is so much different from what I had with Randall. They are like night and day."

"That's not true. Randall and James are the same; it's you and I who are like night and day." Michelle left Amaryllis to her thoughts and soup.

Amaryllis managed to get about three spoonfuls of soup into her belly. She drank the apple juice, then set the tray on the floor and settled down on the bed to watch a movie. She didn't care what her sister just said. No man would have her doing anything she didn't want to do.

When James saw Michelle coming his way, he stretched out his arms to her. She sat down and allowed James to envelop her. "Who's winning, honey?"

"The Vikings got it by seven."

It's not that Michelle cared; she didn't even know what a Viking was. The point of the question was to make James think she was interested.

"Everything okay upstairs?" he asked.

"Yeah, everything's fine."

"I could warm you a plate if you're still hungry."

"No, please don't move. I love being in your arms." Michelle was hungry, but wanted nothing more than to lay her head against his chest.

"What exactly is the matter with your sister?"

"Amaryllis was keeping bad company and it caught up with her." Michelle was very vague in her response, not going into detail about what kind of trouble Amaryllis was in. It was like she was protecting her sister from the outside world.

James was very curious what Michelle meant by *keeping bad company*. He wondered if Amaryllis was into drugs, running from a stalker, or if she was hiding out in Michelle's house from the Chicago Police. Whatever the reason for her being here in Vegas, James respected the fact that Michelle was the big sister to Amaryllis that she needed to be, and evidently, the cause for her visit was to remain personal. He held Michelle tighter in his arms and kissed her forehead.

She laid her head against James' chest and closed her eyes. *Lord, I thank you for my man and I thank you for saving him just for me. You knew exactly who I needed in my life.*

For the duration of the football game, James cuddled Michelle and she fell asleep in his arms.

Chapter 4

On Tuesday morning, James' telephone rang at three-forty five. Having left Michelle's house not too long before that, it seemed like he had just crawled into bed. He sleepily reached for the telephone on his nightstand. "Whoever you are, this better be good."

"When have you ever known a telephone call this early in the morning to be good?"

"Alex, do you know what time it is?"

Alexander Moore had been James' partner as a homicide detective for the past four years. They started out as rookies together and were promoted to detectives at the same time. They were the only two African Americans in the entire precinct. James was leaning more toward dealing with domestic abuse, but Alexander felt the homicide department was more exciting and would keep their adrenaline flowing. After much persuasion for James to come aboard to what he called doing 'real cop's work,' Alexander managed to get him to change his mind.

Their first assignment as homicide detectives was to investigate a case in which a man shot and killed his entire family, then turned the gun on himself. James had never seen so much blood in all his life. And to see children's lifeless bodies made him sick to his stomach. Alexander, on the other hand, was having the time of his life. When Captain Murphy told them both they had to put on latex gloves and check the bodies for pulses, James thought he'd lose his mind. There was no way he was touching a dead body, not even if he were wearing three pairs of gloves, a ski mask and a rubber suit. When the Captain walked away, James turned to his partner. "Alex, I'll give you a sawbuck and a fin if you do this for me."

"James, they're dead. What's the big deal?"

James frowned in disgust. "I don't care, I can't do it, man."

"What are you gonna do when I'm not with you?"

"That's why I thank God we have the same days off, so I don't have to worry about that."

James watched his partner calmly step from body to body, pressing on necks and wrists. He pulled a handkerchief from his pocket, placed it over his nose and mouth, and swallowed saliva repeatedly to prevent himself from vomiting. From then on, each time they left a crime scene, James put cash in Alexander's hand. He figured that as much money as he'd given Alexander, he should be able to claim him as a dependent on his taxes. There wasn't a day that went by that James didn't regret letting Alexander talk him into joining the homicide team, because along with the dead bodies came the telephone calls in the middle of the night.

"Yeah, I know what time it is, James. It's time for us to catch some bad guys. There was a shooting at Marv's Casino. Cap called and said some fool got mad at a slot machine. He claimed it cheated him when it didn't give him all of his winnings. He reportedly confronted the manager of the casino in his office and stated he was owed fifty bucks more. The manager told the guy that the slot machines didn't lie. The next thing anyone knew, two gunshots pierced the air."

James lay on the bed half listening and half asleep. "So, is he dead?"

"As a doorknob, according to Cap. The gunman ran out of the casino. We gotta get over there and view the surveillance tapes."

James let out a loud sigh. "I hate this job; I really do."

"Yeah, well it pays the bills. I'll be at your place in twenty minutes, and don't forget your tie. You know how Cap gets when we're not looking our finest."

"You know, Alex, for the life of me I can't understand why we gotta wear suits and ties to touch dead people and chase criminals. Doesn't Cap realize that gym shoes will outrun a pair of Stacy Adams every time?"

"Well, seeing how Cap is too fat to run himself, he probably could care less."

"I'm gonna have to talk to somebody about this, because it just doesn't make sense."

"Why don't you talk to the person who implemented the dress code?" Alexander suggested.

"That's a good idea. Who is it?"

Alexander chuckled. "Cap."

At the crime scene, James took one look at the casino manager and knew without a shadow of doubt, he wasn't breathing. He presented Alexander with a pair of latex gloves. "Here, Alex, earn your money."

Alexander put the gloves on, knelt over the body and felt for a pulse. He nodded to James, indicating that the man was lifeless.

The city coroner came into the manager's office. "What have we got here, Detectives?"

James was writing notes in his log when he looked up at the coroner. "Just another dead body at four A.M."

Alexander removed his gloves, threw them into the trashcan and walked over to James. "I'm going to get the surveillance tapes, then head to the precinct. Are you rolling with me?"

"Yep, I ain't sticking around here no longer than I have to."

As they were leaving the casino, Captain Murphy called out to James. "Detective Bradley?"

James had accidentally left his necktie at home and thought he was on the verge of being reprimanded. "What's up, Cap?"

"Are you aware that you're wearing mixed matched shoes?"

"Pardon me?"

"Your shoes; they don't match."

James looked down and saw one black Stacy Adam and a brown one. "Sorry about that, Cap. I got dressed in the dark."

"Well, maybe if you had on a black and brown tie, you'd probably make a real fashion statement. Come to think of it, where *is* your tie?"

James could've kicked himself. "I accidentally forgot it, sir."

"You're in violation of the dress code, Bradley. Don't let it happen again."

"I won't, sir."

Captain Murphy looked at Alexander who was tickled at how James was being interrogated. "What's so funny, Detective?"

Alexander immediately straightened his face. "Uh, something I saw on television last night."

Captain Murphy examined Alexander's attire from head to toe. "You got your vest on?"

"I sure do, sir," Alexander said proudly.

Unable to scold Alexander, he decided to let them go. "Carry on, men."

When they turned to walk away, James looked at Alexander. "Someone should tell Cap that jelly stain on his shirt doesn't go with that gray tie."

They both laughed out loud, unaware that Captain Murphy still had his eyes on them.

"What was that, Detectives?" Captain Murphy asked them.

They both looked over their shoulders and answered him under one voice. "Nothing, sir."

By noontime at the precinct, James and Alexander had been hard at work, trying to match mug shots with the face on the surveillance tapes. James was so sleepy and worn out, he didn't know what to do. "Alex, man, I say we call it quits and pick this back up tomorrow morning."

"I'm with you on that, partner." Alexander packed away their files and secured them in a filing cabinet.

Alexander was almost always the designated driver in the company car that was assigned to them. On their way to James' apartment, they drove by a chocolate candy factory.

"Hey, Alex, turn in here. I wanna get Mickey some chocolate covered raisins."

"I thought you were in such a hurry to get home and into bed."

"I am, but I can't see something that my baby loves and

not get it for her." James could have waited until later that evening to give Michelle her candy, but since the candy store and Michelle's law office were both on the way to his apartment, he thought he'd surprise her.

After getting the candy, James and Alexander walked into Price & Associates looking fine and debonair with their dark suits and sunglasses on. In the all-female law firm, James and Alexander were well aware of the many heads that turned their way and the eyes that followed them as they made their way up to the sixth floor.

Chantal, Michelle's secretary, pressed the intercom. "James and Alexander are here. Shall I send them in?"

"Absolutely, Chantal, and hold all of my calls, please," Michelle replied.

Chantal gave them the go-ahead and James walked into Michelle's office with his partner close behind. She stood and walked from behind her desk straight into James' arms.

"Hello, gorgeous," Michelle greeted James.

James embraced the woman he loved then stepped back to admire her beauty. Her hair was parted down the middle and flowing just the way he liked it, and her make-up was flawless, as usual. She wore a red tailor made silk single-breasted pantsuit that looked as though she had been born in it. "You're the gorgeous one, Mickey."

"Not me, you are."

"No, you are," he said.

Alexander looked at Michelle and had to agree with James. "I have to take James' side on this, Michelle; you're absolutely radiant."

"Why thank you, Alex; I'm flattered. What brings you two to my neck of the woods looking like the Blues Brothers in your suits and shades?" She chuckled.

James held up the little white bag he was carrying. "We

were on our way home when we passed a chocolate factory. We stopped and I got you a treat."

Michelle smiled. "You didn't."

"Of course, I did."

She looked inside the bag and squealed. "Chocolate covered raisins, my favorite. Thank you, honey."

James scanned Michelle from head to toe again. "I can't get over how beautiful you look today, Mickey. You are really glowing. Should I be jealous?"

"I can honestly say that you have no reason to be jealous."

James turned to his partner. "Alex, isn't she as fine as she wanna be?"

"And then some, man," he replied.

Michelle sat at her desk to enjoy her treat. "Thanks, gentlemen. I'm due in court in an hour and I wanted to look my best."

James and Alexander each sat down in a chair across from Michelle and watched her munch on the chocolate.

"So, how's your sister doing?" James asked.

"Amaryllis is going to be okay. I'm going to try and get her out of the house tonight. I want the two of us to have dinner with Daddy."

The word 'sister' caught Alexander's attention. "You have a sister, Michelle?"

"Yeah, I thought you knew that," she responded.

"No; James failed to mention it. How old is she?"

"Twenty-six."

"Is she fine?"

Michelle chuckled. "What do you mean?"

"I mean, how does she look?"

"Amaryllis looks just like me, but her complexion is much lighter."

"Then she's fine and I gotta meet her."

James interrupted the conversation. "Slow your roll, partner."

"Look, man, you already have your Eve. I wanna be blessed too," Alexander said.

Michelle ate a piece of chocolate and licked her fingers clean. "Alex, my sister has some issues and a lot of baggage. She's actually here recuperating. I wouldn't recommend you trying to hook up with her, especially right now."

"How long will she be in town?"

"I'm not sure, but it will be a while."

James stood up to leave. "On that note, we're outta here. Kick butt in court today, baby."

"I always do."

Alexander looked at the white bag in Michelle's hand. "Can I have some of your chocolate covered raisins?"

"No," she answered with no shame.

"No? I can't meet your sister, I can't have any of your chocolate. What's up with that?"

"I've already explained about my sister, but as far as my chocolate goes, there are two things that I don't share. That's my man and my chocolate. If you touch either one, you'll surely catch a beat down."

Having said that, Michelle reclined her chair, leaned back and crossed her ankles on top of the desk.

"I was the one driving and didn't have to stop at the chocolate factory."

Michelle still wasn't sharing. "Mmm, but I'm so glad you did. Thanks, Alex."

Alexander looked at James. "How do you put up with her, man?"

"I stay in my place and I don't ask for any of her chocolates," James chuckled.

Alexander shook his head and walked out of her office.

James stepped to Michelle, bent down and kissed her lips. "Call me when court is over."

"You know I will. Where are you headed?"

"Home to make sweet love to my pillow."

"Court is adjourned." When the judge banged his gavel, Michelle heard clapping and turned around to see her father applauding her performance. Nicholas Price was Michelle's biggest supporter. When he wasn't on the golf course enjoying his retirement from Roman Realtors, where he had spent thirty-one years of his life selling homes, Nicholas found himself attending many of Michelle's afternoon court sessions. He admired the way she could be firm, yet gentle, when the need arose. Michelle was the type of attorney that gave her clients their money's worth.

"Well done, daughter, well done," Nicholas said proudly.

Michelle greeted her father with a hug and smile. "Thanks, Daddy. I always do my best."

"And it shows. After you finished your closing argument, I looked at the defense attorney and could tell by his expression that he knew he didn't have a leg to stand on."

Just then the defense attorney approached them and spoke to Michelle. "Excuse me, Counselor. It's not often that I do this, but I wanted to commend you on your performance this afternoon. I have to say that you've certainly done your homework regarding this case. I tip my hat to you. Congratulations."

Michelle often received praise and admiration for her courtroom conduct, but having her father there to witness this man's words, put joy in her heart. "Thank you, Counselor, and might I say that it was a pleasure beating you." She smiled.

He smiled in return. "And beat me you did. If you don't mind me asking, where did you go to school?"

"I attended Oxford University."

From his suit jacket pocket, he presented Michelle with his business card. "Oxford, that's quite impressive. If you're ever in need of a job, look me up. I'm sure the partners at Levin & Bell would be interested in knowing what you have to offer."

Nicholas placed his palm over his mouth to try to conceal his smile because he knew his daughter was about to blow this man's mind and he was glad he could be there for this proud moment.

Michelle couldn't be rude. Though she didn't need it, she accepted his business card. "Counselor, I happen to *own* Price & Associates. I have partners working for *me*. My *performance*, as you call it, was for the benefit of the young lady sitting behind me. She's the newest attorney to join my firm. She was here to see how I want my law firm represented. So, I'll turn the tables and tell *you* that if *you're* ever in need of a job, look *me* up." Michelle looped her arm through her father's and sashayed out of the courtroom, leaving the defense attorney speechless.

"Baby Girl, you get more and more like me everyday," Nicholas said.

"What can I say? It's in the genes."

Nicholas walked Michelle to her SUV and opened the door for her. "So, how's Amaryllis?"

"She's fine, Daddy."

"Have you told her that you wanted the three of us to have dinner this evening?"

"No, not yet. I'm hesitant a bit. Daddy, Amaryllis thinks you're going to come down on her for the way she lives, but I don't want you to do that. She's here trying to get herself together. So, instead of chastising her, I want you to do the opposite. I know it may be difficult, considering all the things Amaryllis has done, but I really feel the best thing to make your relationship with her better is to encourage her. She's willing to let bygones be bygones if you are."

"So, The Bad Seed wants to let bygones be bygones, huh?"

"And that's another thing, Daddy. You have to stop calling her that. Why kick Amaryllis when she's already down?"

"Because that's exactly what she does to other people. But I blame her mother for that. Veronica taught Amaryllis to behave that way. And I'm gonna be honest with you, Michelle, I don't think it's a good idea for her to stay in your house."

"Daddy, Amaryllis is my sister. Why would you say something like that?"

"Call it a hunch, but if I were you, I'd put her up in a hotel. Las Vegas has plenty to choose from."

"That's ridiculous. I have four bedrooms, what reason do I possibly have to put my own sister in a hotel?"

"Look, Baby Girl; you know your sister's track record as well as I do. You know what she's capable of. Don't underestimate Amaryllis. She's known for taking folks' kindness for weakness."

"Daddy, listen to me. I've talked to Amaryllis and she understands the way she's been living is wrong. I believe she really wants to get her life together and we have to be her support system."

Nicholas threw his hands in the air. "Okay, it's your house and your call, but I'm telling you that I have a strange feeling in my gut that she's up to something. I just hope your hospitality doesn't end up biting you in the butt."

"Everything will work out, Daddy; you'll see. Besides, what could Amaryllis do to me?"

"Baby Girl, let's pray we never find out."

Amaryllis was coming down the stairs when Michelle and Nicholas walked in the front door. Michelle placed her purse and briefcase on the sofa and went to assist her sister down the last three steps. "Hi, sweetie, it's good to see you getting around. Guess who's here?"

Amaryllis looked at a man whom she hadn't seen or talked to in two years. Their relationship was strained. Neither of them had picked up a telephone to talk to one another in the past twenty-four months. "Hi, Daddy."

Nicholas looked at the healing black eye, the stitches sewn in the corner of her mouth, the cast that held up her right arm and the cane she was leaning on. "What in the world happened to you?"

Amaryllis was puzzled and looked at Michelle. "You didn't tell him?"

"It wasn't my place, Amaryllis. That's for you to do." Michelle left Amaryllis and Nicholas alone and went into the kitchen, heading toward the refrigerator. She opened it and didn't see what she wanted to see and screamed at the top of her lungs. Nicholas and Amaryllis were both startled and saw Michelle run back into the living room waving her hands in the air like a mad woman. She stood in front of her sister and yelled. "Did you eat my Chunky?"

Amaryllis looked at Michelle like she was a lunatic. "Uh, yeah."

Michelle's eyes were blaring. "Why?"

"I wanted a snack."

"There are cookies, chips, doughnuts and all kinds of junk in the pantry. Why did you eat my Chunky?"

"I didn't see a name on it, Michelle."

"In the short time you've been here, have you brought any food into this house? Everything in the kitchen has my name on it. Please stay away from my chocolate."

Amaryllis was fed up with her. "Michelle, is it that serious? I'll buy you another Chunky. Just shut up."

"Look, Amaryllis, I'm going to lay down the rules about my chocolate. If you touch it again, you'll be on your way back to Chicago so fast you won't need a plane, because my foot will be your transportation." Michelle grabbed her purse from the sofa and stormed upstairs.

"Well, can I at least have some of your double chocolate ice cream with the brownies in it?" Amaryllis teased.

Michelle stopped in her tracks and looked at Amaryllis then pointed her right foot toward her. "You're gonna find yourself airborne, okay? I ain't to be played with about my chocolate." Michelle turned her attention toward Nicholas. "You better talk to her, Daddy."

They heard Michelle's bedroom door slam. Nicholas looked at his youngest daughter and her bruises. "Who did this to you?"

"I got into something that I shouldn't have, but don't worry. I've learned my lesson."

"The guy you were living with; did he do this to you?"

"No, Randall wasn't a fighter, and I'd rather not get into this with you. I don't wanna hear the I-told-you-so speech."

"I just wanna make sure that you're really okay."

"Yeah, I'm fine now that I'm here. Michelle's been taking good care of me."

"It's nice of your sister to accept you into her home and nurse you back to health, isn't it?"

"Yeah, Michelle's been great."

Nicholas gave her a stern look. "Remember that, Amaryllis."

Michelle came down the stairs dressed in blue jeans, a white tank top and dark blue wedge heel sandals. "Okay, I'm ready."

"Ready for what?" Amaryllis asked.

Michelle had waited all day to tell Amaryllis about their dinner plans. She figured Amaryllis wouldn't reject in the presence of their father. "You and I are going out to dinner with Daddy."

Amaryllis was uncomfortable with Nicholas' last words. She felt as though he had threatened her. "You and Daddy go ahead, Michelle, I don't feel so good."

Michelle pressed the back of her hand on Amaryllis' forehead. "What's wrong, are you sick?"

"I just don't feel like going."

Nicholas knew that he put something on Amaryllis' mind, and that's exactly what he had meant to do. "Maybe you'll feel better if you eat something," he said to Amaryllis.

Michelle looked at her. "What have you eaten today besides my Chunky?"

Amaryllis rubbed her stomach. "Nothing. I really haven't had much of an appetite."

"But I bet you've been swallowing those pills, haven't you?"

"I took two this morning, but I was able to stay awake all day."

Michelle was pleased that the Tylenol she switched with the Vicodin was much gentler to Amaryllis' system. She grabbed Amaryllis gently by her waist. "You're coming with us. I see I'm gonna have to spoon feed you like an eight month old."

Oh great, Amaryllis thought. The last thing she wanted to do was sit in the company of her father over a dinner table. Amaryllis hated sports, but she'd rather stay at home and watch a boring tennis match than sit for two hours listening to Nicholas praise Michelle on her achievements in life.

Chapter 5

Wednesday morning, Michelle sat behind her desk speaking into a Dictaphone when Chantal walked into her office, all smiles. A week ago, Chantal had shared with Michelle that she'd thought she could be pregnant. Chantal and her husband, Douglas, had been trying for five years to conceive. In spite of all of the fertility treatments that she'd been subjected to, Chantal's womb had still been without child. Today, Chantal's menstrual cycle was more than two weeks late, and Michelle allowed her the morning off to visit her gynecologist in hopes of receiving wonderful news. But it was the smile on Chantal's face that told Michelle that God had answered her prayers.

Michelle placed the Dictaphone on the desk and stood up. "Well, what's the verdict?"

Chantal threw her hands in the air and yelled at the top of her lungs, "I'm pregnant!"

Michelle hurried around the desk and wrapped her arms around her personal secretary of two years. "Oh, my God. Congratulations, honey."

"Michelle, I can't believe it. Douglas and I have been trying for so long and it finally happened. For five years the doctor's told us to give up trying because it would never happen."

"This just proves that doctors don't always know what they're talking about. And the saints of God have connections with the Head Physician. Can I get an Amen?"

Chantal laughed. "Amen, girl; amen."

"Does Douglas know?"

"No, I didn't even tell him that I thought I might be pregnant because it would only hurt him again if it turned out that I wasn't."

"You're glowing already and you look so happy."

"Michelle, I heard my baby's heartbeat today. I can't tell you what that felt like. There's a life inside of me being nurtured by everything that I do. I feel so, so, so . . ."

Michelle found the word Chantal was searching for. "Overjoyed?"

"Yes overjoyed; that's the word."

Michelle sat in one chair and motioned for Chantal to sit in the one opposite her. "Let's sit for a minute because I wanna share something with you."

"Good, 'cause I wanna share something with you too," Chantal said.

The two women faced one another, and before Michelle could utter one word, her emotions were already running rampant. She took hold of Chantal's hands and fought back tears that were threatening her lower eyelids. "I've known you for two years, and for those two years, I've watched you get excited when your period was late. I've also witnessed the disappointment, month after month, after month, when you had to face the false alarms. You and I have prayed and cried many a day, but I want you to know how happy I am that you and Douglas will finally become parents. I wish you both all the happiness in the world and I know if there were ever two people on this earth who will make excellent parents, you and Douglas fit the bill perfectly."

Chantal was rendered speechless. What could she say after that? She had wanted to share her own thoughts and feelings with Michelle. Tears spilled out of her eyes like a waterfall. She silently prayed for God to give her the strength she needed to speak to Michelle.

"Michelle, I'm so grateful that I have a saved boss," Chantal started. "You've been so supportive. I remember coming to you after leaving the doctor's office crying and wanting to have a pity party, but you never let that happen. You took me by the hand and brought me in here and we got on our knees and called on the name of Jesus. You don't know how much that kept me sane. If it weren't for you, I would have lost my mind a long time ago."

Through her tears, Chantal saw Michelle's. "I thank you for always being in my corner and not letting me give up on God when I wanted to. I especially thank you for threatening to send me home without pay that time I told you that I didn't want to come into your office and pray about my situation."

They both laughed and Chantal kept on sharing. "I was actually angry with you for getting in my business, but now I can see that God has placed you in my life for that particular reason. I can't thank Him enough for sending me you, my angel. I love you, girl."

Just when Michelle thought she couldn't cry anymore, even more tears fell down her cheeks. "Oh, Chantal, you don't have to thank me. But I have to be honest and tell you that you got on my nerves feeling sorry for yourself, but I did what I had to do to keep you strong. It wasn't easy holding you up, but God gave me what I needed in order to do what I had to do. I won't even bother telling you how much I fasted on your behalf for God to hurry up and bring this baby forth; 'cause you won't believe me. I actually gave up chocolate for a whole week for you and you know that you must be someone special for me to do that, 'cause I don't even give up chocolate for my own issues."

Chantal put her arms around Michelle and squeezed her tight. "I appreciate you for giving up the chocolate."

"You'd better," Michelle teased.

Chantal brought a serious expression to her face. "There's something else I need to tell you." She looked into Michelle's eyes with a sullen expression. "I've gotta take a leave of absence, effective immediately."

Michelle's eyes grew wide. "What? Why?"

"I'm six weeks pregnant, but I'm already three centimeters dilated, which means that my cervix will have to be sewn shut at ten weeks to keep the baby from making his or her appearance too soon. My doctor wants me on complete bed rest until I'm seven months, and at that time, I'm gonna have to be induced because the weight of the baby will be too heavy on the stitches."

Michelle wore a horrid expression. "Seven months? Isn't that too early to deliver?"

"Well, my doctor says that chances are good that the baby's lungs will be developed enough so that he or she can breathe on its own. We may be able to wait longer than seven months, but that depends on the weight of the baby. I promised him that I was on my way home and into bed, but I just had to come by here and tell you about my miracle first."

"Well, in that case, go home and get into bed."

"What about the Henderson case? I didn't finish typing the brief on it. I was gonna finish it this afternoon."

"That's no longer your concern, Chantal. You are officially on maternity leave; now go home," Michelle demanded.

"But what about—"

Michelle shooed Chantal out of her office. "What about nothing. Go home and relax. I'll call you later, then you can fill me in on everything that needs to be completed for the Henderson case."

"Michelle, I hate to leave you like this when so much is going on. What are you going to do without a secretary?"

"I'm going to cry, but I'll figure something out. I don't want you worrying about that."

"If I take my laptop home with me, I could work in bed."

"Are you crazy, Chantal? That's not a bad idea, but are you crazy? The only thing you should be concentrating on is what color to paint the nursery."

Michelle helped Chantal carry a few personal things to her car after she had finished packing up her desk. "How will you tell Doug the good news?"

"I think I'll bake a cake and put *Congratulations, Daddy* on it and sit it on the kitchen table."

"Oh, I like that. Make sure to call me when you both come down from the high and tell me about it."

Chantal hugged Michelle one last time. "I will, and thanks for everything."

Michelle stood in the parking lot and watched as Chantal's car disappeared from her sight. "Lord, I thank you for Chantal's miracle, but what am I gonna do without my secretary?"

"Hey, sis," Michelle greeted.

Amaryllis was lying on the sofa watching her favorite channel when Michelle walked in the front door with more paperwork than she could carry.

"What's all that?" Amaryllis asked.

"My secretary took a sudden leave of absence today and this is all the stuff she left behind. I've gotta be in court in the morning and I need to type a brief before then."

"Can you type?"

Michelle set the paperwork on the cocktail table, plopped down on the sofa next to Amaryllis and exhaled. "Not a lick. I'm probably at fifteen words a minute."

Amaryllis laughed at her. "Michelle, fifteen words a minute isn't typing, that's pecking. Let me see what you got."

That was the first time Amaryllis had laughed since she'd been in Las Vegas. Michelle noticed her stitches in the corner of her mouth were absent. "Hey, you can laugh. I forgot you were going to get your stitches removed today. Please tell me that you decided not to call a taxi and let Daddy take you to the doctor I had recommended."

"Yes. I relented and allowed him to play his role. But I can tell that Daddy doesn't like me. He didn't say two words to me the entire time on the way to the doctor's office or on the way home. He didn't even ask how my visit went. I wish you hadn't made me go to dinner with you two Monday evening. He ignored me the whole time. If it weren't for you carrying the entire conversation and forcing him to acknowledge me from time to time, Daddy would've treated me as though I was invisible."

Michelle was well aware that Amaryllis had been a thorn in their father's side ever since she could utter her first words. Like oil and water, the two of them just didn't mix.

"You know, Amaryllis, I don't know what to say about you and Daddy. You're both behaving like children. Why won't you be the bigger person and address the issues the two of you have?"

As far as Amaryllis was concerned, Nicholas was the father and he should be the one to approach her if there was to be a reconciliation. She ignored Michelle's question and focused on the large amount of paperwork her sister dumped on her lap. "All of this has to be typed for court tomorrow?"

Michelle let out a loud sigh. "All of that."

"I'll do it for you. It should take me no longer than two hours."

"Amaryllis, there's no way you can do that in two hours."

"Correction, there's no way *you* can do it in two hours. I'm on a leave of absence as an administrative assistant for a law firm in Chicago."

"Oh, my goodness. I completely forgot about that. But do you feel up to it? You've only been here a few days. How's your shoulder?"

"It's getting better and better every day. It's been a month since the incident and now, I've gotten rid of my cast and cane. Except for an occasional ache, my shoulder is fine."

"Amaryllis, if you can get this done for me, I'll love you forever."

"You've got to do that anyway."

"I'll love you forever and a day, how about that?"

"I like that better."

Amaryllis emerged from Michelle's home office one hour and twenty minutes later. Michelle was lying on the couch half asleep when Amaryllis placed the brief on her lap. She sat up and looked at it, then looked at her sister. "What's this?"

"Your brief."

"You're done?" Michelle asked scanning the typed pages in amazement.

"Yeah, I told you it wouldn't take that long. It's what I do."

"Amaryllis, I can't believe you were able to complete all of this so quickly. How fast are you?"

"Approximately seventy-eight words per minute."

Michelle's wheels were turning. "Do you feel well enough to be put on my payroll?"

"Yeah, I think it's about time I got back into the swing of things."

"Great, you're hired and you start tomorrow morning at eight o'clock. What was your pay in Chicago?"

"Michelle, I don't expect to be paid. You've already done so much for me. Room and board is more than enough."

"Amaryllis, nobody in their right mind works for free. Of course I'm going to pay you. Besides, your story will change once you see all the duties Chantal had. She was my right hand woman who practically ran the firm in my absence."

"Speaking of Chantal, she called right before you came home."

"Great, I'll call her, then you two can talk. I'm sure she wouldn't mind briefing you on what you need to know. I pay her twenty-eight dollars an hour. Is that suitable for you?"

"You pay your secretary that much, Michelle?"

"Chantal's worth it. I couldn't function without her. She's my eyes and ears."

"Heck yeah, that's suitable. It's a whole lot more than I was making in Chicago. You better be careful, Michelle, you're spoiling me. I may never leave you now."

"You're my sister, girl. I love having you here. I just hope you can handle the work load."

* * *

After just three hours behind Chantal's desk, Amaryllis was fit to be tied. Michelle said that Chantal had her hands full, but she didn't tell Amaryllis that she was a superwoman. Back in Chicago, all Amaryllis had to do was pay Bridgette to take the load off of her, but here in Reno, she was on her own. No wonder Michelle paid Chantal so generously. Looking at all of the work, Amaryllis thought Chantal was probably underpaid.

At noontime, Amaryllis took a break and looked away from the computer screen. She had to blink about three or four times to correct her vision. Her fingers were cramped and her legs were numb from sitting in one position for way too long.

Michelle came out of her office and approached Amaryllis. "How's it going, honey?"

Amaryllis was in a funky mood and decided to tell her sister a thing or two about abusing employees. "Let me tell you something, Michelle. All this work you have Chantal doing is ridiculous. No wonder she took an early leave. And I bet she was paying someone on the sly to help her out." Amaryllis held up her fingers for Michelle to see them. "Look at my fingers; they're crooked."

Michelle caressed Amaryllis' fingers. "Come on, it's not that bad, is it?"

"It's worse than bad. How could Chantal handle all of this?"

"I don't know, but she did. And thanks for typing that brief for me last night."

"You're welcome. What time do you have to be in court?"

"Three o'clock this afternoon. Has James called?"

"No, he hasn't called at all today."

Just then the elevator doors opened and James stepped off displaying a picture perfect smile and a dozen roses in his hand. He walked straight to Michelle and kissed her lips.

"Hello, gorgeous."

Michelle smiled at his smile. "You're the gorgeous one."

"Not me, you are."

"No, you are." Michelle turned to her sister. "Amaryllis, this is James, the love of my life. James, this is my baby sister, Amaryllis." She was so happy to finally introduce the two.

James took a single rose from the dozen and presented it to Amaryllis. "Here's to the second most beautiful woman in the world. It's my pleasure to meet you, Amaryllis."

Amaryllis took the rose from him. "What a gentleman. Thank you, James."

"You're not letting Mickey work you too hard, are you?"

Amaryllis wiggled her fingers. "That's an understatement. I've been typing since eight o'clock this morning and now I can't feel my fingers or legs."

James gave Michelle the remaining eleven roses. "These are for you, and you should be ashamed of yourself."

Michelle inhaled the scent from the roses. "Amaryllis is a professional, she can handle it."

James looked at Amaryllis sympathetically. "Sorry, I tried." He grabbed Michelle's free hand and kissed the back of it. "Have you eaten yet, beautiful?"

"Not yet. I was just about to ask Amaryllis if she wanted to go to lunch."

"Looks like I'm just in time, then. I'll treat you both to a nice juicy steak. How about it, Amaryllis. Are you up to it?"

"I appreciate the offer, but I've got too much work to do," Amaryllis replied.

Michelle was grateful to Amaryllis for helping her out, but she certainly didn't want her to think that she was being taken for granted. "Sis, I don't care how much work needs to be done, I never expect you to work through your lunch or your breaks. I think it would be great if you come to lunch with us."

"Thanks again, guys, but to be honest with you, I just don't feel like going to a restaurant."

"Are you sure?" James asked.

"Yeah, I think I'll go next door to the deli and get a salad," Amaryllis said.

Michelle ran a soft hand across Amaryllis' sore shoulder. "Okay, but I expect for you to spend your entire lunch hour relaxing. Why not go to the employees' lounge on the second floor and put your feet up?"

"That's sounds like a good idea; maybe I will."

James withdrew a twenty dollar bill from his wallet and gave it to Amaryllis. "Since you're not dining with Mickey and me, enjoy your salad on me."

Amaryllis was in awe at the kindness of this man. "You don't have to buy my lunch, James."

"Even though you're not eating with us, I'd still like to treat you today." James smiled.

Amaryllis placed the money in her wallet. "Thanks, I appreciate it."

Michelle gave Amaryllis the bunch of roses she was holding. "Can you put these in water and place them on my desk for me?"

"Of course I can. Have a good lunch." Amaryllis stood up.

When James and Michelle got to the elevator, he turned around. "Can we bring you anything back?"

He was smiling and Amaryllis could see his dimples. James was handsome and a complete gentleman. He treated her sister with the utmost respect and Amaryllis understood why Michelle was crazy about him. She focused on his dimples and smiled back at him. "No, thanks."

When the elevator doors closed, Amaryllis sniffed her single rose and thought to herself, *He's in love with Michelle and she barely lets him touch her. I wonder if he's content with that. A man like James shouldn't be deprived.*

She placed Michelle's roses in a vase and filled it with water, then set the vase on Michelle's desk next to James' picture. She picked up the photograph and looked at his smile. "No, you shouldn't have to be deprived, James."

The telephone rang and she sat down at Michelle's desk to answer it. "Price & Associates, Amaryllis speaking."

"What's up, ghetto fabulous?"

"Bridgette, I left you a message on your voicemail for you to call me here three hours ago. What took you so long to call me back?"

"Amaryllis, when it's ten o'clock your time, it's twelve noon my time. I was at lunch."

"Oh yeah, I forgot about the time difference."

"What was so urgent?"

"I was trying to do a spreadsheet and I needed you to talk me through it, but I figured it out. What's new with you?"

"Ain't nothing new with me. My life is always the same; boring. Wait a minute, why are you doing spreadsheets? It just dawned on me that the number you left for me to call you at is to your sister's firm. You took your tail to Vegas and got a job, Amaryllis?"

"I'm just helping out Michelle. Her secretary is on a maternity leave."

"Well, isn't that special? The partners still haven't hired a temp to come in and take your place, so I got double the workload. I'm telling you, I'm two seconds away from walking out of this place without looking back. I haven't been to the riverboat casino to get my gamble on since you've been gone. But that's enough about me, are there any cute guys in sin city?"

Amaryllis looked at James' picture again. "There's this one guy who has potential."

"Ooh la la. Who is he?"

"Someone who would be perfect for me, but he's not available."

"Let me guess. He's married, right?"

"Nope, engaged."

"Engaged doesn't mean untouchable," Bridgette replied.

"It kinda does, Bridgette."

"Excuse me. Who am I talking to? The Amaryllis I know *always* gets her man. Have you gotten soft on me, girl?"

Amaryllis laughed. "I must have, because back in the day I would've pursued any man whether he was married, engaged or whatever."

"Yeah, you've certainly broken up your share of marriages and relationships, girlfriend."

"I know, and I wanna leave that lifestyle behind, but there's something about this guy that jumps out at me. Today, he brought me a rose and invited me to lunch, but I turned him down," Amaryllis said sadly.

"Because he's engaged?"

"Yeah."

"Well, how in love can he be with his woman if he's buying you flowers and asking you to lunch?"

"That's what I need to find out. Just how much in love is he?" Amaryllis wanted to know more for herself than for Bridgette.

"What's his name and how did you meet him?"

"His name is James and my sister introduced us. He's a

homicide detective, and according to Michelle, he's deeply rooted in his church."

"Another church boy, huh?"

"He's a minister, Bridgette."

"A minister? Come on now, Amaryllis. You should know by now that you and church boys don't mix."

"I know, I know. I don't do well with church boys, but for James, I might consider going to church."

"Okay, I don't wanna bring up the past or anything, but I gotta know; Randall was a church boy and darn near perfect. So, what's so different about this James guy that you'd be willing to go to church?"

"I can't answer that. Like I said, it's just something about him."

"Well, in that case, do what you gotta do to get your man, Amaryllis."

"It might just come to that, Bridgette. Me doing *whatever* I gotta do."

Chapter 6

"Court is in recess." The judge banged his gavel and left the courtroom.

Michelle felt a tap on her shoulder and turned to see her father. "Hi, Daddy."

"Baby Girl, you were phenomenal, as usual."

"Thank you, but I'm frustrated right now." Michelle looked at her wristwatch.

"James and I were supposed to meet at my house this evening to select the wording for our wedding invitations. I really hadn't planned on being in court this long."

"Well, you heard the judge's ruling, so there's nothing you can do about it. Just call James and tell him that you're stuck in court."

"Okay. Are you leaving now?"

"Yeah, I've gotta pick up Margaret. We're going to the opera tonight."

Michelle was happy that her father had met a woman he enjoyed spending time with. Margaret Ayers, a widow and a retired librarian, was perfect for Nicholas. Golf was her passion as well. She and Nicholas had met on the greens three months ago and have been inseparable ever since.

Michelle took to Margaret the moment Nicholas introduced the two. Michelle thought she was kind and warmhearted. "If I wasn't able to witness this, Daddy, I wouldn't believe it. I can't picture you sitting in a theatre enjoying opera."

"I hate it, but Margaret loves it and I love her, so I do what I gotta do. It's called sacrifice. You know where I'm coming from, Baby Girl?"

"Absolutely. You taught me well. Say 'hello' to Margaret for me."

Nicholas kissed his daughter's cheek and left the courtroom. Michelle took her cellular phone from her purse and called the precinct.

"Homicide; Detective Moore speaking."

"Hi, Alex; it's Michelle."

"Hi, yourself. What's up?"

"Please tell me that James is still there."

"Sorry, you just missed him. As a matter of fact, he's on his way to your house. So, tonight's the big night, huh?" Alexander knew that James and Michelle were getting together at her house to select wedding invitations. James had been talking excitedly about it all day.

"Well, it was supposed to be, but I'll be stuck in court longer than I thought. I'll try reaching him on his cell."

"That won't do you any good. He left it at home this morning."

Michelle exhaled a sigh of frustration. "I hate it when he does that. Thanks, Alex."

"So, Michelle, uh, what's up with your sister? When can I meet her and why are you hiding her from me?"

"Alex, I told you my sister has some issues, and now is

not the time for her to get involved in a relationship with anyone."

"I just want to meet her."

"And then what, Alex?"

"Nothing."

Michelle knew better than that. "Yeah, right. Amaryllis is my secretary these days. You can come by the office and introduce yourself."

"Okay, cool." Alexander didn't hide the fact that he was excited.

"Alex, I'm going to say this to you and you can take it anyway you want. Amaryllis Price ain't nobody's punk. My advice to you is to keep your distance, but if you want to stick your hand in the cookie jar, you just might pull out a bullet."

"What the heck does that mean? Are you saying that if I get involved with your sister, it would be like committing suicide?"

"All I'm saying is that you've been warned, and whatever happens between you two, I don't wanna know about it."

"Is she a psycho or something?"

"You ain't heard it from me." Michelle chuckled, ended her call with Alexander and called home.

"Price residence," Amaryllis answered after the second ring.

"Ooh, I like that. How are you doing, sis?"

"I'm okay, where are you?"

"I'm stuck in court for God knows how long. James and I were supposed to get together this evening, but I can't get a hold of him to tell him that I won't be home until much later than expected. So, when he gets there, please apologize for me. And tell him I love him and maybe we can get together tomorrow night."

"Okay, no problem."

As soon as Amaryllis placed the telephone on its receiver, it rang again.

"Price residence."

"Hello, gorgeous."

At the sound of James' voice, Amaryllis' heart skipped a beat. "Hi."

"That's not the way we do it, Mickey. You're supposed to tell me that I'm the gorgeous one."

Gorgeous you are, baby. "This is Amaryllis."

"Oops, my bad. You and Mickey sound exactly alike. I can never tell you two apart when you're on the telephone."

"Everybody says that." Amaryllis chuckled.

"Is my beautiful fiancé there?"

It was nothing for Amaryllis to tell a lie. "She called and said that she's running late. She's stuck in court, but she wants you to come over anyway and wait for her. She shouldn't be too much longer."

"Okay, that's cool. Hey, have you eaten yet?"

"No, I haven't."

"I can stop and pick up dinner. What have you got a taste for?"

I got a taste for you. "I'm not sure. What have *you* got a taste for?"

"To be honest with you, I can go for soul food. Maybe meatloaf and mashed potatoes with gravy. I wouldn't mind corn on the cob and grape Kool-Aid."

As he was speaking, the wheels in Amaryllis' head were turning. She remembered the conversation she had with Michelle about cooking for men. Michelle wouldn't cook meals like that for James often because she felt that he'd get spoiled and would eventually stop appreciating her good gesture. But Amaryllis knew all too well that a home

cooked meal was a straight path to a man's heart. She remembered cooking meals for Randall on a daily basis,
and he treated her like a queen. "You know, James, I can
cook that for you here."

"Girl, you can burn like that?"

"Oh yeah, I can do a little something in the kitchen."

"I don't wanna put you through any trouble, Amaryllis. I
know you're still recovering."

"Don't be silly, it's no trouble at all. Come on over. By
the time Michelle gets home, dinner will be ready."

"Thanks, Amaryllis. I had to stop at home and get my
cell phone, so I'll be there in about an hour."

Amaryllis called a seafood restaurant and ordered a
dozen raw oysters on a half shell for delivery. Her mother
once told her that oysters were aphrodisiacs, and if she
fed them to a man, he'd instantly be under her spell.

She managed to honor James' request. The meatloaf
was tender and juicy, the mashed potatoes were buttery
and lump free, the corn on the cob was hot and ready and
the grape Kool-Aid was chilling in the refrigerator. The
raw oysters sat in a tray on the table next to the meatloaf.

After a steamy shower, Amaryllis styled her hair into a
French roll then took a stroll into Michelle's closet and selected a pink chiffon teddy that was meant for God's eyes
only. She sprayed Michelle's Ralph Lauren perfume behind her ears and went downstairs to the kitchen where
she lit two candles and dimmed the kitchen light. The bait
was set. Just as Amaryllis was finishing setting the table,
the doorbell rang.

"It's show time," Amaryllis whispered under her breath.
She opened the door to see James standing there with
pink carnations and a small white bag in his hand. He
looked at Amaryllis from head to toe and had to blink his

eyes a few times to make sure he was seeing what he thought he was seeing.

The pink chiffon teddy hugged her every curve and it left nothing for his imagination. He was stunned and couldn't move. Amaryllis reached for his hand and pulled him inside. "You're just in time, James. Dinner is ready. I hope you're hungry."

James started to sweat. He'd never been in this situation before and he didn't know what to do. "Uh, what's going on, Amaryllis?"

"Just dinner."

"Why are you dressed like that?"

"What? This? This is something I just threw on." Amaryllis turned around to give James a rear view. "Do you like it?"

"Where's Mickey?," he asked nervously.

"I told you that she's gonna be late."

James looked at his wristwatch. It was almost 5:30 P.M. Surely, court couldn't be in session this late in the evening. "I thought she would've been here by now."

Amaryllis could see the flowers shaking in his hand. "Do I make you nervous?"

"Nah, I'm cool," he lied. James was as nervous as a hooker sitting on the front pew in church. Not only were his hands shaking, but his knees were getting weaker by the second.

"Are those flowers for me?" Amaryllis asked.

"No, I bought them for Mickey."

"What's in the bag?"

"Chocolate squares for Mickey."

Mickey, Mickey, Mickey. All this talk of Michelle was getting on Amaryllis' last nerve. She took the flowers and candy from James. "I'll make sure she gets them. Come on into the kitchen. I lit candles and I ordered oysters for an appetizer."

James didn't move from where he stood. He may have been a minister, but he'd heard about oysters and the effect they supposedly had on men. "Uh, Amaryllis, I don't think this is a good idea."

"What do you mean?"

"The way you're dressed; I don't think Mickey would appreciate it."

"This ain't about Michelle, it's about you and me."

James frowned. "What are you talking about? There is no you and me."

"But what about the rose you gave me today, and calling me beautiful?"

"You *are* beautiful, Amaryllis. I gave you a rose because you're my fiancé's sister, but I'm in love with Michelle."

Amaryllis stepped to James and put her arms around his neck. "But she can't give you what I can give you, James. I know you two aren't sleeping together."

James was shocked that Michelle would share such personal information. He removed Amaryllis' arms from around his neck and took a step backward. "She discussed that with you?"

"Oh, yeah. Michelle told me everything. And a fine man like you should be fulfilled."

"Look, Amaryllis; whatever you had planned to happen tonight, ain't going down. And I'm sorry if I gave you the impression that I was interested in you. Michelle is the one I love." James opened the front door to leave.

Amaryllis was stunned that her beauty and perfectly planned evening didn't impress James. "So what am I supposed to do now?"

He turned and looked at Amaryllis. "That's on you, but I'm not down with this." James shut the door behind him, got in his car and drove straight to his pastor's house.

Bishop Joel Graham opened his door and saw a distraught James. James had been his armour bearer and right hand man for the past six years. Bishop Graham and his wife, Cookie, didn't have any children of their own, so when James became his armour bearer, they treated James as if he was their own son. "What's wrong, Son?"

"Bishop, you won't believe what just happened." James walked past him and sat down on the living room sofa.

Bishop Graham sat in his La-Z-Boy recliner across from James. "You act as though you've just seen the devil."

"You have no clue how right you are." James stood and began pacing the floor.

Cookie came into the living room from the kitchen. "Everything okay in here?"

James approached his first lady and kissed her cheek. "I'm sorry to disturb you, Cookie."

"You're not disturbing us, James. You know you're always welcome here. You want some dinner?"

"Nah, I just stopped by to talk to the Bishop about something."

"Okay, then I'll leave you two alone."

James had his mouth all set to enjoy soul food, and whatever Cookie had cooked tonight was penetrating his nostrils. When she turned to walk away, James called out to her, "Um, what did you cook?"

"I baked beef spareribs and I got garlic mashed potatoes and pinto beans."

The hunger in James' stomach was singing a song. "Could you make me a plate to go?"

"Sure, but I want my Tupperware back because it ain't the cheap stuff."

"I hear you, and I promise to return it."

"I'll leave it on top of the stove for you." Cookie winked at her husband. "Call me if you need anything."

Bishop Graham smiled at his wife but didn't say anything. James caught the chemistry between them. "Bishop, it amazes me how the two of you are still so much in love with each other after twenty years of marriage."

"Cookie is the apple of my eye," he admitted, his dreamy smile confirming such.

"I can tell."

James placed his hands in his pockets and started pacing the floor again. Bishop Graham reclined his chair, folded his arms across his chest and watched James for a full sixty seconds. "Whenever you're ready, James, just jump right in. I prefer you do it before you wear a hole in my carpet."

James sat down on the sofa and looked at his Bishop. "I don't know where to begin."

James proceeded to tell him what happened at Michelle's house that evening. Bishop Graham listened to his story, and the only thing he could say was, "Wow."

"Wow is right. Now you gotta tell me what to do because I have no clue." James looked at his Bishop with worry in his eyes.

"Well, son, the first thing you do is to tell your fiancé'."

James would rather be crucified than tell Michelle. "Bishop, there is no way I can tell Mickey about this. Give me something else."

"Don't be a fool, James. You've gotta tell Michelle and you definitely wanna get to her before her sister does."

"Uh-uh. Mickey would have a fit. Who do you think she'll believe, me or her flesh and blood?"

"James, listen to me. You and Michelle love each other and are planning a wedding.

You can't allow this to come between you. If you sit her down and tell her exactly what happened, I'm sure she'll see her sister for who she really is."

James stood, put his hands in his pockets and paced the floor again. "I don't know, Bishop. Mickey loves her sister. You should hear the way she talks about her. 'My baby sister this' and 'My baby sister that.' "

"She loves you too."

"I know, but I don't wanna hurt her. If I tell her about this, she'll either hate me or hate Amaryllis. The bottom line is she'll be hurt and I can't do that to her."

"James, you're about to mess up. You and Michelle have been together for a long time. You told me her sister has only been in town barely a week. Do you really think she'll find you at fault?"

"I can't risk my relationship, Bishop."

"You're risking it by not telling her what happened. You don't want this woman to get to Michelle first and tell another version other than what really happened, because I guarantee you that her sister's version won't be anything nice. And guess who's gonna look like the guilty party? You."

"Amaryllis is living with Mickey rent free and she's working at the firm."

"So?"

"I don't think she'll tell Mickey anything because she wouldn't want to mess that up."

"James, you're gambling with your relationship. Michelle loves you and I'm sure she'll believe you."

James's cellular phone rang and he saw Michelle's home number. He stopped pacing and looked at his Bishop. "It's Mickey, what should I do?"

"I already told you."

He answered his phone. "Hello, Mickey."

"Hey, gorgeous," Michelle said on the other end.

"What's up?" James asked nervously.

"What did you say?" she asked.

"I said, what's up?"

"Something is wrong, what is it?"

James looked at his Bishop as he answered Michelle. "What do you mean?"

"You didn't greet me right. Now, tell me what's wrong."

He could've kicked himself. When Michelle greeted James, he didn't tell her she was the more gorgeous one of the two. "Nothing's wrong, baby. Everything's cool."

"Where are you?"

"I'm at Bishop's house."

"Why?"

"I stopped by to talk church business."

Pastor Graham looked at James and shook his head from side to side.

"Amaryllis told me you came by. I'm sorry I wasn't able to reach you to tell you that I'd be stuck in court all evening and couldn't meet you tonight." Michelle sounded regretful.

"You were gonna tell me not to come over?"

"Yeah, I talked to Alex and he told me that you had left your cell phone at home, so I called Amaryllis and told her to tell you that I couldn't make it."

"Amaryllis said that you wanted me to come over and wait for you."

"I don't know how she got that mixed up, but what about the wedding invitations? You wanna come back over and take a look at them?"

"Now?"

"Yeah, now. It's still early."

James's wristwatch told him that it was almost 6:30 P.M. He thought it was too early for Amaryllis to have gone to bed. He didn't want to interact with her again. In fact, if James never saw Amaryllis's face again, it would be too soon. "Um, you know what, Mickey? I'm kinda tired and I really wanna just go home and get into bed. Can we do it another time at my place?"

Michelle knew her man well and something was definitely bothering him. "James, baby, talk to me. What's wrong?"

"Where's Amaryllis?"

"Amaryllis? She's upstairs in her room. Why?"

"Did you get the flowers and candy I left for you?"

"Yes. She put the flowers in water and the candy was on the kitchen table next to the flowers. Thank you."

James thought about the candles and oysters. "Did you see anything else on the table?"

"Just a dinner plate Amaryllis wrapped up for me. That reminds me, she said she offered you dinner but you said you didn't wanna eat."

Because that's not all she offered. "You talked to her?" James questioned.

"She said you told her that you didn't like meatloaf and I know that's not true. So, why didn't you stay and eat?"

He had to come up with a logical excuse fast. "Because the Bishop called and asked if I could stop by. Since I didn't know how long you were gonna be, I decided to come by and see what he wanted."

Bishop Graham looked at James in awe and couldn't believe the lie he was telling, and to include his name was totally wrong.

"But you could've eaten before you left. I know how much you love a good home cooked meal, James."

That statement reminded James not to forget the meal Cookie had set aside for him. "Well, I wasn't really hungry and I didn't want to eat without you."

"I think you hurt Amaryllis' feelings, honey. She was kinda upset that you didn't stay and eat. She was just trying to be nice to you."

Yeah, nice and easy, James thought.

"James, are you there?"

"Yeah, baby, I'm here. Listen, the Bishop and I are done talking, so I'm gonna head home."

"Are you sure everything's okay? You sound kinda funny."

"Yeah, everything's cool. I'll call you tomorrow."

"Okay, sweetie, I love you."

"I love you too, Mickey."

James ended the connection with Michelle and saw how his Bishop was eyeing him. "I know what you're going to say."

"So, I'll say it anyway. You're gonna regret not telling Michelle what happened."

"Amaryllis didn't say anything either, so maybe this will all blow over." James was hopeful.

"James, I love you like a son and I pray that you'll take heed to what I'm saying. You've got to tell Michelle what her sister did."

That was not an option for James. "No, I can't do it."

"What if this woman comes after you again?"

"Then I'll put her in her place."

"But what if she doesn't stop? You can nip this in the bud now. Don't let this manifest into something bigger. You are really underestimating Michelle's love for you and her intelligence. And you better hope and pray real hard that she doesn't ask me about that lie you told about me calling you over here."

"It just really ticks me off that Amaryllis has placed me in a position where I have to lie to Mickey."

"Amaryllis didn't put you in a position to lie, you've made that decision all on your own, son."

James walked to the door then turned to his Bishop. "Can you get my dinner for me?"

"In this house, liars get their own dinners."

James walked into the kitchen and returned with the Tupperware bowl. He got to the door and paused. "I appreciate your time, Bishop."

"You can mess around and let the devil destroy your relationship if you want to, but I advise you strongly to do the right thing and tell Michelle before it's too late. I *will* say 'I told you so' before I try and help you fix the situation."

James didn't respond. He walked out the door and gently shut it behind him, not even giving his Bishop's advice another thought.

Chapter 7

Two days later, on a Friday morning, James exited the elevator and walked straight into Michelle's office without acknowledging Amaryllis sitting behind her desk. As soon as James closed the door, Amaryllis went to Michelle's office door and pressed her ear against it to eavesdrop.

Michelle stood up and practically ran into James' arms. "There's my gorgeous man."

He squeezed Michelle so tight he almost took her breath away. "I keep telling you that you're the gorgeous one, Mickey."

"Not me, you are."

"No, you are."

Michelle kissed his lips. "This is something we'll never agree on."

Amaryllis listened as they complimented each other. She was fed up with this 'you're the gorgeous one' crap. Who cared about all of that? Every time Michelle and

James got together, they drove her nuts with their petty game. One would think they were two teenagers the way they carried on.

Michelle had better have her fun now, because Amaryllis was getting ready to nip that 'gorgeous' thing in the bud.

Michelle wrapped her arms around James's neck. "What brings you here?"

"I stopped by to ask you for a huge favor."

"How huge?"

"Not real big huge."

"Small huge?"

"I'm hoping you'll see it that way."

Michelle went back to her chair and sat down then looked at him. "Okay, lay it on me."

"Alex and I are flying to Detroit to fetch two bad guys we've been looking for. For the past six months, they've been on the move. Apparently, they were hiding out in Motown and thought they had gotten away scot-free until they were spotted in a nightclub. And since it's our case, we've got to do the fetching."

"What did they do?"

"Let's just say that women will be a lot safer without these two goons walking the streets."

"Oh, I see. But what has this got to do with a favor from me?"

"I've got carpet cleaners coming out this evening to get a grape juice stain out of my carpet in the living room. I was hoping you'd let them in for me because Alex and I won't get back until late tonight. It has taken three weeks to get this appointment and I really don't wanna cancel. Please say you'll do it."

Michelle got up, walked around the desk and sat in his lap. "What time?"

"The appointment is for five o'clock this evening."

"Okay, I'll do it for you. I'm due in court at eleven this morning and I'm sure I'll be done by then."

James kissed Michelle on the lips. "Thanks, babe, I owe you one."

James gave Michelle access to his apartment. "This big key is for the main door, and this silver one is for my top lock. The gold one is for my bottom lock."

On the other side of the door, Amaryllis made a mental note of which key went to which lock.

"James, please be careful with these men. I don't wanna have to hurt anybody for messing with my baby."

He pulled Michelle into his arms. "I love the way you love me, Mickey."

"If she loved you, she'd make love to you," Amaryllis mumbled under her breath. She heard footsteps and hurried back to her desk. She sat down and began typing on her keyboard.

James exited Michelle's office and was walking when he stopped and turned around. From his interior suit jacket pocket, he withdrew something large, squared and wrapped in silver paper foil. He tossed it to Michelle. She caught it and gave James the widest grin when she saw what it was.

"Ooh, a Chunky. My baby knows what I like." Michelle smiled.

"There's more where that came from. I'll call you later." He closed Michelle's door behind him and completely ignored Amaryllis. He went straight to the elevator and pressed the 'down' button.

Amaryllis' eyes followed him and she admired the way James' suit framed him. She'd give anything to see those biceps and triceps that were bulging through the linen. And tonight she may get her chance to do just that.

"Hey, Detective, you want to have a little fun with your

handcuffs?" Amaryllis teased. "We could play 'cops and robbers' and I'll let you lock me up."

The elevator doors opened and James stepped into it and turned to face Amaryllis. "You're sick, you know that?"

The elevator doors closed and she sat there hot and bothered. James was playing hard to get real well, but that night, Amaryllis had plans to break him all the way down.

On a yellow sticky note, Amaryllis wrote down the information about James' apartment keys then folded it and put it in her purse.

Just then, Michelle came from her office. "Hey, sis, I'm on my way to meet Daddy for brunch before heading to the courthouse. You ought to come with me. You could see your big sister do her thang."

"Nope, don't feel like being bothered with Daddy today. He irks me."

Michelle exhaled. "Amaryllis, you and Daddy have got to get it together."

"Tell *him* that," Amaryllis said, giving Michelle much attitude.

Michelle exhaled a sigh of frustration, put her purse on her shoulder and walked to the elevator. "You know what? I'm not gonna let you two stress me today, I'll see you later."

As soon as Michelle was out of sight, Amaryllis hurried into her office to look for James' keys. She frowned when she didn't see them on the desk. She walked around and opened Michelle's center drawer and saw one big key, a gold key and a silver key. She snatched James' keys then grabbed her own keys and purse and walked to the elevator.

* * *

Fifteen minutes later, Amaryllis exited a hardware store with her own set of keys to James' apartment. She crossed the street and entered a beauty supply store, finding just what she was looking for, sitting on a Styrofoam head on one of the store's shelves.

A sales lady approached her. "May I help you?"

"Yes, how much is that long blond wig?" Amaryllis pointed. After the woman stated the price of the wig, Amaryllis became the owner of it.

Ten minutes later, Amaryllis walked into 'Snap To It', and purchased a small camera with a timer. She had one more stop to make. From the moment Amaryllis walked into the pharmacy, it took a half hour for her name to be called.

The pharmacist handed over Amaryllis' prescription. "I'm sorry about the wait, Miss Price, we had to call Chicago to get your doctor's approval."

Amaryllis returned to the law firm with everything she needed. She placed James' original keys back in Michelle's center drawer then sat down at Michelle's desk and called Bridgette in Chicago.

"Parker & Parker Law Offices, Bridgette speaking."

"Hey, girl, it's me. I called to tell you that I'm getting ready to get my man." Amaryllis was excited.

"You mean you're getting ready to get someone else's man."

"Whatever." She wasn't about to let Bridgette rain on her parade.

"When is this going to take place?"

"If I play my cards right, I could sneak in James' place and set everything up before he gets home tonight."

Bridgette chuckled. "Set everything up? What are you gonna do, film a movie?"

"Something like that. I gotta wait for Michelle to do her thing first."

"Your sister, Michelle? What's she got to do with anything?" Bridgette wondered out loud.

"Oh, Bridgette, I didn't tell you. James is Michelle's man." Amaryllis was nonchalant in her confession.

Bridgette was typing, but she stopped and gave Amaryllis her full and undivided attention. "Say what?"

"You heard me."

"Amaryllis, is this the same man you told me about before? The detective? The minister?"

"Yep."

"And he's your sister's fiancé?"

"One and the same," Amaryllis answered, not even caring that her upcoming plans for James would devastate Michelle.

"Okay, you've done some wild stuff in your day, but this is totally off the chart, even for you. You didn't tell me this guy was your sister's man. What are you thinking?"

"I'm thinking about how good it's going to feel laying in his arms tonight."

"Do you hear yourself, girl? He's your sister's fiancé. *Hello?*" Bridgette couldn't believe Amaryllis' gall.

"And?"

"And what you're doing is wrong."

"Bridgette, you're the one who told me to do what I gotta do to get my man."

"Fool, that was before I knew he was marrying your sister. You left that part out when you told me about him, you nut ball."

"Well, now you know. I need to get off of this phone and plan my evening right."

"Don't you hang up on me, Amaryllis. This will destroy

your relationship with Michelle. You do know that, don't you? She's your only sister and she loves you. You haven't even been in Vegas two weeks, and already, you're acting the fool. How can you live in her house, work for her and do this behind her back?"

Amaryllis looked at James' photograph and traced his smile with her finger. "Easily."

Michelle and Nicholas were just finishing eggs and bacon when her cellular phone rang. "Michelle Price speaking."

"Miss Price, this is Yolanda Cooper with Blessed Events Consulting. I'm calling to see if you and your fiancé have decided on the wording for your wedding invitations. With the wedding just two months away, now is the time to place your order."

"Hi, Yolanda. Yes, we've decided, and I'm sorry that I didn't get in touch with you sooner. I'll have my secretary fax our selection to you right away. It's not gonna be a large ceremony, so we'll only need one hundred invitations."

"Alright, Miss Price, I'll look for the order on the fax machine."

Michelle ended the call and looked at her watch. "Daddy, I've got to get over to the courthouse, but I want to know if you've decided on wearing a white tuxedo or a black one."

"Baby girl, I'll wear whatever you want me to."

"I prefer white. Is that okay?"

"Whatever you want. How much are the wedding invitations?" Nicholas asked.

"Only about one hundred dollars or so."

Nicholas reached in his pocket and pulled out a wad of bills.

"What are you doing, Daddy?"

"Giving you the money for the invitations."

Michelle was pleased at her father's generosity, but she and James had decided that they would cover all the expenses for their wedding. "James already paid for them."

Nicholas put the cash away and withdrew his checkbook from his interior pocket of his suit jacket and started to write.

"Now what are you doing?"

"Writing James a check."

"Daddy, that's not necessary, James and I can take care of everything."

"Michelle, I can afford to pay for my daughter's wedding, okay? It's what fathers are supposed to do." Nicholas tore the check out of the checkbook and gave it to Michelle. "Give this check to James and tell him that you're still my responsibility until you're pronounced husband and wife, so don't overstep his bounds. He's lucky I'm letting him have you at all. I wanted you to be a nun."

Michelle chuckled. "Oh well, you still have one daughter left. Maybe you can turn Amaryllis into a nun." She thought about what she just said and wished she hadn't.

Nicholas looked at her and shook his head from side to side. "Now that's funny. Amaryllis a nun? That'll be the day."

"Daddy, I wish you would cut her some slack. Amaryllis has been on her best behavior since she's been here in Vegas. How do you think it makes her feel when you praise me and frown at her? And please stop calling me Baby Girl when she's around, because it hurts her feelings. She's your youngest daughter, not me."

"Listen, Michelle, a leopard like Amaryllis can't change her spots. I told you that I've got a gut feeling that she's still living foul. We just can't see it."

"She's not doing anything, Daddy. Amaryllis isn't the

one keeping up mess, you are. And I'm surprised at your behavior."

"And I'm surprised you let your guard down with her."

"I trust my sister."

"You know the song, *Open My Heart* by Yolanda Adams?"

"Yes, I have the CD."

"In the beginning of the song, Yolanda asks God 'What if I choose, the wrong thing to do?' You need to ask yourself that same question, Baby Girl."

"And why is that?"

"Because choosing to trust your sister is *the wrong thing to do.*" Nicholas sang the last five words to Michelle the same way Yolanda Adams sang them.

Michelle stood up to leave. She put the check Nicholas had given her in her purse, then gathered her things and looked at her father. "Amaryllis has faults just like the rest of us. No one is perfect. And it would be nice to have you in her corner instead of being on the opposite side of the ring with your boxing gloves on, ready to take a jab at Amaryllis every chance you get. Now, I want you to really think about what I've just said to you, Nicholas Price. I'm on my way to court. I'll talk to you later."

She kissed her father on the forehead and left the restaurant. He sat at the table and watched Michelle walk away, wondering if she could be right about Amaryllis. Was he being too hard on her? For some reason, he just couldn't shake his gut feeling about her.

Michelle got in her Jaguar and called the firm.

"Price & Associates, Amaryllis speaking."

"Hi, honey; it's me," Michelle greeted.

So what? "Hi."

"I need you to do something for me."

Like what, sex your man? "Sure, what is it?"

"In my top file cabinet drawer, there's a manila folder marked 'Invitations.' Inside, you'll find the wedding invitation that James and I selected. Can you please fax it to the number that's on the front of the folder, to Yolanda Cooper's attention?"

Fax it yourself. "No problem, sis. I'll take care of it right away."

"That's why I love my sister; you always come through for me. We gotta get these invitations ordered and in the mail soon."

"Why waste your time? There ain't gonna be a wedding," Amaryllis said to herself after she ended the call with Michelle.

She went into her sister's office to retrieved the manila folder. She read the wedding invitation. The wording was beautiful and everything was fine except one thing, and she knew how to correct it. She took the invitation to her desk and opened a bottle of liquid paper and covered Michelle's first and middle names. She blew on it to dry it, then inserted the invitation into her typewriter. In place of Michelle's name, Amaryllis typed her own name.

Satisfied with the wording, she called Blessed Events Consulting. "Hi, this is Michelle Price. May I speak with Yolanda?"

"Hi, Michelle. This is Yolanda. What can I do for you?"

"My secretary is faxing my wedding invitation to you, but I want to make you aware of a small change. I want to use only my second middle name instead of Michelle Denise."

"That's fine, Michelle, whatever you wanna do. What's your second middle name?"

"It's Amaryllis, and can you please make sure that it's spelled correctly? I've already made the change; you'll see it on the fax."

"Okay, Michelle, but what made you change your mind about your name?"

"I like Amaryllis better. It matches perfectly with James."

After ending the call, Amaryllis read the invitation again before faxing it.

I hold you in my heart for we have shared together
God's blessings.

Philippians 1:7

Mr. Nicholas Price
requests the honor of your presence
at the marriage of his daughter

Amaryllis Price
to
Minister James Bradley

On Saturday, the sixth of December
Two thousand and nine
at two o'clock in the afternoon

Praise Temple Church of God
1751 Grace Parkway
Las Vegas, NV

The trail winds onward through the hills from here to
prairie's end; will our journey ever last? As long as
you're my love, my friend.

To God be the glory for what He's done!

Amaryllis faxed the invitation, covered her name with liquid paper and retyped Michelle's name. She made a copy, shredded the original, then inserted the copy in the manila folder and placed it back in Michelle's file cabinet.

Of course, Michelle would be upset at what her sister had done, but Amaryllis couldn't care less.

Chapter 8

At 4:30 P.M., Michelle stepped off the elevator, rushing into her office.

Amaryllis looked at the clock on the wall. "Where are you going in such a hurry?"

"I've got to get over to James' place and I'm running late." She grabbed James' keys and rushed back to the elevator. "How late are you staying?"

"Not too much longer. I was talking to some of the ladies in the lounge today and they were telling me that there's this book club they've got going on. They meet once a month at each other's homes. Tonight, they're meeting again and I was thinking about going."

"Sweetie, I think that's wonderful. It's about time you got out of the house and started mingling."

Oh, I'll be doing much mingling tonight. "Then I'll go ahead and join them, so don't wait up."

"Okay, I won't. What book are they reading this month?"

"Something by Victoria Christopher Murray, I'm not sure what the title is."

"My friend Jodie loves her books."

Amaryllis looked at the clock and it read 4:35 P.M.. "Well, you better hurry up. You don't wanna be late meeting the carpet cleaners."

Michelle looked at her curiously. "How did you know why I was going to James' place?"

She had to think of something fast. "Uh, when James stopped by earlier, I asked him what brought him by and he told me."

"Oh. Well, I'm on my way. Enjoy your book club meeting."

At 6:20 P.M., Amaryllis was parked on the corner of Michelle's block. She sat in Michelle's Lincoln Navigator, watching the Jaguar enter into the garage at the town home. Michelle had done a lot for her sister. Not only had she given Amaryllis room and board, she'd also given her the keys to her SUV. Michelle never worked a straight 9 to 5. And she was in and out of the office much too often for them to carpool.

As soon as Michelle closed the garage door, Amaryllis started the Navigator and pulled away from the curb. On the passenger seat, she had James' address written on a piece of paper. Amaryllis had stolen James' information from Michelle's Rolodex that sat on her desk. When she arrived in front of James' apartment building, Amaryllis glanced at the yellow sticky note to familiarize herself with which key went to which lock.

Inside his apartment, Amaryllis put her plan into action. She rushed into the kitchen and opened the refrigerator. Just as she expected, James had a full pitcher of grape Kool-Aid, his favorite drink, sitting on the top shelf. She set the pitcher of Kool-Aid on the table and opened the bottle of Vicodin she'd gotten from the pharmacy, pouring twenty of the twenty-five pills on the table. An empty mayonnaise jar from James' dish rack became an instant grinding tool.

It took Amaryllis fifteen minutes to change the pills to a fine powder. When that was accomplished, she added the powder to the pitcher of Kool-Aid, then placed the lid on the pitcher and shook it vigorously for five minutes before placing it back on the top shelf in the refrigerator. She rinsed the mayonnaise jar and dried it with a paper towel, then returned it to the dish rack. She placed the bottle with the remaining five pills in her purse and cleaned the table as best she could.

In the living room, Amaryllis loaded the film into the tiny camera and hid it on the window ledge between two large potted plants. She went into James' bedroom and undressed. When she saw his black satin sheets hugging his mattress, she couldn't resist the temptation. Amaryllis climbed into his bed, completely naked, and made herself comfortable. She smelled a familiar fragrance and pressed her nose into his pillow.

Instantly, she was reminded of Randall. Boss was his favorite cologne and he wore it well. Amaryllis was having a good time rolling between James' sheets. It had been a long time since she'd been in a man's bed, and she was glad to be back where she figured she belonged.

She stopped rolling and looked up at the ceiling, imagining herself lying on James' chest. She closed her eyes and pictured him touching her body in all the right places. After a while, Amaryllis was so caught up in this dream that she passionately called out James' name, and it was her own voice that had awakened her.

She nervously sat up and saw that it was dark outside. James' alarm clock read 8:35 P.M. and she realized that she'd actually fallen asleep. Amaryllis jumped out of bed and made the satin sheets look the way James had left them. The telephone on his nightstand rang and it startled Amaryllis. His answering machine picked up after three rings.

"Hello, you've reached the home of James Bradley. Leave a message after the beep and I'll get back to you ASAP."

At the sound of his voice, Amaryllis got goose bumps all over.

"Hey, gorgeous one. Just calling to see if you were home yet. I pray that everything went well in Detroit. You'll be pleased with the carpet. I think they did a great job. If it's not too late when you get in, give me a call. I love you."

Michelle's telephone call infuriated Amaryllis. She heard James tell Michelle that *he* would call *her* when he got back home from Detroit, so why couldn't Michelle just wait for that? Why did she have to call and interrupt Amaryllis' flow?

"You might as well go to bed, Michelle; James won't be calling you tonight."

Amaryllis went into the bathroom, brushed her hair in a circle around her head and put on the blond wig. She placed the brush in her bag, then took the bag and all of her belongings and placed them under James' bed. In the kitchen, she double checked and made sure there were no traces of white powder on the table. Next, she walked into the bathroom to check for long strands of hair in the sink. In the living room, she made sure that she'd removed all traces of her being there. She went back into the bedroom and crawled under the bed to wait for her prey.

Amaryllis couldn't have timed this evening any better;

five minutes after she crawled into her hiding place, James entered the building.

Amaryllis' heart started to race when she heard James turn his key in the first lock. Under the bed, she waited in anticipation. The only thing she could think about was the Kool-Aid. Everything would go so smoothly if he'd just drink a glass. But she had a plan B. If James didn't drink any of the Kool-Aid, she'd hit him over the head with something heavy to knock him out. The choice was his. James could make this easy on himself if he was thirsty.

The first thing James did was pay a visit to his bathroom. A couple minutes later, he walked into the bedroom and listened to his messages. After hearing Michelle's voice, he sat down on the bed and called her. Amaryllis saw the phone jack on the wall and wanted nothing more than to snatch the cord from its socket.

"Hello, gorgeous. Not me, you are."

Amaryllis' skin was crawling with anger. Again, Michelle was messing up her flow.

"Yeah, I just got in a minute ago and got your message . . . I missed you too, baby. Yeah, I saw the carpet . . . I didn't think the stain would come out. At least now I can keep my security deposit when I move in with you . . . I can't wait either."

I can't wait for you to drink that Kool-Aid, Amaryllis thought as she waited.

"I'm gonna hop in the shower and hit the hay. It's been a long day. Did you order the wedding invitations?"

"No; I did," Amaryllis mumbled.

"Amaryllis? I hope she didn't screw it up."

You're the one that's about to get screwed, James.

Before James ended his call with Michelle, he said a prayer with her that God would continue to bless their relationship. "Call me when you get to the firm tomorrow. I love you too, Mickey. Good night."

Yeah, good night, Mickey.

James went into the bathroom and started the water in the shower. Back in his bedroom, he undressed. Amaryllis could only see his ankles and feet, but tried her best to scoot closer to see the rest of him without making any noise. She couldn't do it though. She'd just have to wait on the Kool-Aid to take effect.

While James was showering, she heard him singing a gospel song. Before he came back into the bedroom, Amaryllis got in a position that would allow her to see *all* of James from where she was. After singing three verses of the song, James exited the shower, dried himself and entered his bedroom.

"Ooooh, weeeee," Amaryllis whispered. Seeing James naked from head to toe made her wonder how Michelle could abstain. Then again, she probably wouldn't know what to do with him anyway.

James sat on the bed and applied lotion to his body. When he was good and moisturized, he stood and walked out of the bedroom. Amaryllis saw the back of him and had to put her hand over her mouth to conceal her excitement.

She heard James moving around, but couldn't tell what he was doing. She hoped James was having a drink of the grape Kool-Aid. She didn't want to have to use a blunt object to knock him out, but she would if she had to.

Two minutes later, James came back into the bedroom, opened a drawer for a pair of boxers and put them on.

Amaryllis figured James wouldn't need any boxers tonight.

He left the bedroom again and Amaryllis heard the refrigerator open and close. She heard what sounded like a glass being set on the table. She heard what sounded like liquid being poured into the glass and knew it was the Kool-Aid. About two minutes later, she heard the glass being set in the sink, then she heard the refrigerator open and close again.

Good boy, she thought.

James came back into the bedroom, turned out the light, then walked into the living room and sat on the sofa. He turned on the television and lay back on the couch. He didn't see the small camera that was on the window sill directly in front of him. Amaryllis patiently waited a half hour for the Vicodin to take effect. When she figured enough time had passed, she crawled out from under the bed, went into the living room and stood in front of him.

"James?" She whispered his name. He didn't stir. She called him again, this time a little louder. "James?" When he didn't move, she tapped him on the shoulder. "James?"

Amaryllis lifted his left eyelid and he still didn't move. She turned off the television then turned on the living room light. She stood in front of James again and looked at his triceps and biceps that she'd been longing to see all day. "Ump, ump, ump, I don't know how you could stay away from this, Michelle."

Amaryllis carefully removed James' boxers and positioned him on the couch where the camera would catch his entire body. She set the camera for ten seconds and climbed her naked body on top of him with her back to the camera. She placed James' hands on her breasts. When she heard the camera snap, she climbed off of James and set it for another ten seconds then climbed on James again, this time bending forward, placing her lips on his. Her mission was accomplished. Amaryllis had done exactly what she came to do.

Before she dressed James in his boxers, Amaryllis got a good look at his naked torso and wondered again how Michelle could be so strong willed. She dressed James in his boxers then turned the television on and the living room light back off. She grabbed the camera and gathered her things from under the bed and got dressed. Amaryllis went into the kitchen and got the pitcher from the refrigerator and poured the Kool-Aid down the sink. She rinsed the pitcher and made a fresh batch of grape Kool-Aid. Afterward she placed the pitcher back in the refrigerator, then rinsed the glass that James had drunk from. She took all of her belongings into the living room and stood in front of James and looked at him lying there helpless, and looking mighty delectable. She bent down and kissed his lips then left his apartment.

Amaryllis drove the Navigator into the garage and entered the town home. When she got to the second floor, on her way up to the third, Michelle opened her bedroom door and stepped into the hallway. "Hey."

What is she doing up? "Hi."

"How was the book club meeting?"

"It was nice." Amaryllis wanted nothing more than to get out of Michelle's presence.

Michelle folded her arms across her chest and leaned against her bedroom doorway.

"So, which book by Victoria were they discussing tonight?"

Amaryllis searched her brain for an answer. "You know what, Michelle? I forgot to even ask. We were so wrapped up in the discussion that it didn't dawn on me until I was on my way home that I didn't even know the name of the book. But I'll ask one of the ladies tomorrow."

"Who hosted the meeting this month?"

I don't know. What difference does it make? "Uh, that new girl that works in the file room. Uh, uh . . ."

"Jessica Taylor?"

"Yeah, Jessica."

"That was nice of her to invite all of you to her home. Jessica's only been at the firm for a month."

"Yeah, it was nice of her." Amaryllis feigned a yawned. "I'm kinda tired, so I'm gonna head on up. I'll see you in the morning."

Michelle walked up to Amaryllis and kissed her on the cheek. "I love having you here. I hope you'll stay on after the wedding. I'm sure James wouldn't mind the three of us sharing this place until you can find a place of your own if you decide to make this move a permanent one."

"We'll see. Newlyweds should live alone the first year."

"But you and I are just starting to get close again and I don't wanna lose the closeness we have."

Amaryllis couldn't say anything. She gave Michelle a slight smile and turned to walk away.

"Amaryllis, is everything all right?"

Guilt was trying to creep in but Amaryllis fought it off like penicillin attacking an infection. "Yeah, why do you ask?"

"You seem distant. Did anything happen tonight that I should know about?"

Amaryllis's heart started to race. "I'm just tired. It's been a long day."

"It's funny that you'd say that, because James said the same thing to me."

Amaryllis's fingertips got cold. "Goodnight, Michelle." Amaryllis walked up the stairs to her bedroom. Of all nights, why did Michelle want to hold a conversation *this* night?

Once inside her bedroom, Amaryllis stripped from her clothes and got into the shower. She thought about Michelle's offer, but the last thing she'd want to do was live with her and James. "By the time I get finished, Michelle, you'll be asking if you can stay with *me* and James."

Chapter 9

Friday morning, James was awakened to banging on the door.

"James, are you in there?"

He lazily sat up on the sofa. It took him a moment to figure out where he was. He looked around and wondered what he was doing in the living room. The banging on the door got louder.

"James, open up, man."

He looked at the door and frowned. "Alex?"

"Yeah, man; open the door."

James slowly stood and staggered to the door. He opened it and saw Alexander standing in the hallway. "What are you doing here?"

Alexander saw that James appeared to be lethargic and bewildered. "Man, what's up with you? Now I know why you didn't wanna carpool with me today. You weren't coming in to the precinct at all, were you? Do you know that it's eleven o'clock? Roll call was four hours ago. And why are you answering the door in your drawers?"

James looked down at his attire then looked at Alexander through sleepy eyes. "Man, I honestly don't know."

"You look like crap."

"I feel like it too. Come on in."

James stepped aside and Alexander walked into the apartment. Alexander sat down on the sofa. James stood by the door with one hand on his waist and the other on his chin, looking up at the ceiling as though he was trying to figure out something.

Alexander followed James' gaze but didn't see anything. "What are you looking up there for?"

He looked at Alexander. "I was getting ready to do something, but I forgot what it was."

Alexander saw that James was behaving erratically. "Are you high, partner?"

"Why would you ask me something like that?"

"Because you look high."

James looked up at the ceiling again. "What was I getting ready to do?"

"How about get dressed and save your job? You're AWOL."

"What time is it?"

Alexander looked at him like he was insane. "Didn't you hear me say that it's eleven A.M.?"

James looked at Alexander in shock. "It's eleven o'clock?"

Alexander got up and stood in front of James. "We're partners, man, and we've had each other's back for a long time. Talk to me. Why are you trippin'? Did you smoke a little something last night?"

"Alex, get out of my face. I must have jetlag or something."

"Or something is more like it."

James looked at the ceiling a third time. "I feel like I need to do something, but I don't know what it is."

Alexander worked his hands like he was doing sign language and spoke. "You need to go to work. Get dressed and let's go."

James left Alexander alone in the living room while he went to get dressed. Clearly James wasn't himself this morning. Alexander sat on the sofa again and glanced around James living room for drug paraphernalia. There had to be a reason James was acting abnormal.

An hour later, James and Alexander walked into the precinct and instead of going to his desk, Alexander went toward the stairs.

"Where are you going, Alex?" James asked.

"Downstairs to see if any of the marijuana is missing from evidence; 'cause you're trippin'." Alexander continued his plight.

Before James could say anything else, Captain Murphy was in his face.

"Good morning, Cap," James greeted.

"You mean afternoon, don't you, Detective?," Captain Murphy asked, scanning James from his head to his shoes. "So, you decided to come to work, huh? Why weren't you at roll call this morning?"

"Well, see, what had happened was, uh, this morning, I mean last night, the storm knocked the power out and my alarm clock didn't ring."

"What storm?"

"You know, the storm, that big storm, uh, . . . it didn't storm in your neighborhood?"

"No, it didn't," Captain Murphy answered looking deep into James' eyes.

"Oh." James searched his brain for another convincing lie. "Well, uh, a squirrel or a raccoon or a possum or a cat, something got tangled up in the power lines outside my apartment. When that happens, the power goes out and then my alarm clock doesn't ring."

Captain Murphy gave James a look to let him know he didn't believe either lie he had just told. Just then, a female officer called the Captain's name. He looked over his shoulder and motioned for her to wait a minute then brought his attention back to James. "You better be glad I'm in a hurry, Detective."

"You have no idea how glad I am, sir."

"Don't play with me, Bradley. I ain't in the mood. I'll have your badge."

"Yes, sir."

He looked at James' neck. "Where's your tie?"

James felt for a tie that wasn't there and could've kicked himself. "Uh, see, what had happened was, it was dark in my closet because someone ran into the light pole outside and knocked the power out and I couldn't find—"

"Cut the crap, Bradley, and find that no good partner of yours and get over to the crime scene on Logo Street."

Captain Murphy walked away and James let out a loud sigh just as Alexander was coming up the stairs from the evidence room.

"Did you find what you were looking for?" James asked him.

"Yeah, it's all there and you better be glad too."

"What do you mean I better be glad?"

"You're on something, James, and I'm gonna find out what it is."

"Yeah, whatever."

"I saw Cap walk up to you. What was he talkin' about?"

"The same thing he's always talking; a bunch of ying yang. Come on, we gotta get over to Logo Street."

"Why?"

"Because someone's lying dead on it."

Early afternoon, Amaryllis stood at the counter at the Photo Mart. "Can this film be developed today?"

"Sure, it'll be ready after six P.M.," answered the store clerk.

"Is that special still on, the one that allows you to make an eight by ten puzzle from any picture?"

"Yes, it is."

"Great. I want the first photograph made into a puzzle."

Back at the law firm, Amaryllis was sitting behind her desk when James and Alexander stepped off the elevator. James walked past Amaryllis without speaking, and headed straight into Michelle's office. She watched James shut the door behind him. She looked up at Alexander smiling at her. *Who is this clown?* she thought.

As if Alexander heard her thought, he extended his hand toward Amaryllis. "Hi, I'm Alexander Moore; James' partner."

Amaryllis took his hand and shook it. "Hi, I'm Amaryllis. Michelle's sister."

"It's a pleasure to meet you. Michelle mentioned that she had a sister and I've been wanting to meet you."

Amaryllis was not impressed. Alexander's presence was irritating her. Because of him, she couldn't eavesdrop on Michelle and James' conversation. "Is that so?"

"Yes. And you are as beautiful as Michelle said you were."

Tell me something I don't know. "Thank you, Alexander."

He smiled. "My friends call me Alex."

"Thank you, Alexander. So, what's up with your partner?"

It didn't go over Alexander's head that Amaryllis repeated his full name. Evidently, she didn't want to be his friend. "What do you mean?"

"He walked right by me without speaking."

"For some reason, James has been out of it today. Don't pay him any attention. If you asked him what his name was, he wouldn't be able to tell you."

"Oh, well if you'll excuse me, I've got to get to the file room."

Amaryllis stood and walked past Alexander. He waited for her to disappear from his view before he knocked on Michelle's door. He peeped his head in and saw James and Michelle sitting across from one another. "Is it safe to come in?"

Michelle looked at him and smiled. "Of course, Alex. Come on in," she said.

He walked in and shut the door behind him. "I just met your sister and she's great—beautiful, too."

James didn't say anything. He looked at Alexander as he came and sat next to him.

"So, you're digging my little sister, huh?" Michelle asked Alexander.

James thought to himself, *You're digging yourself into a grave.*

"Yeah, she's cool. And she's even prettier than I pictured," Alexander answered.

"Oh, yeah; Amaryllis is absolutely gorgeous," Michelle stated.

Amaryllis may be beautiful on the outside, but to James, her inner person was very ugly. "You're the gorgeous one, Mickey," he stated.

Alexander turned to James. "You've gotta admit they can pass for twins. A yellow beauty and a brown beauty.

Michelle chuckled. "Everyone tells us that. When I look in the mirror, I see Amaryllis' face."

"She's got your smile, your hair, your face and you two are built exactly the same. You even have the same voice," Alexander described.

James had come to visit with Michelle, not to sit and compare her with her evil sister. "Well, I don't see any resemblance at all."

Alexander begged to differ. "Man, you're crazy. They're identical."

James was getting madder by the moment. "They're not identical, Alex. They're years apart." James spoke with authority and it caught both Michelle and Alexander's attention.

In the year they'd been dating, Michelle had never heard him speak in that tone. "Is something bothering you, sweetie?"

Before James could answer her, the telephone rang. By the fourth ring, Michelle pressed the intercom button. "Amaryllis, could you get that please?"

Alexander leaned forward. "She went to the file room."

On the fifth ring, Michelle answered. "Price & Associates, Michelle speaking. Hey, Jodie; what's up, girl?"

While Michelle was talking on the telephone, Alexander glanced at James. "What's up with you, man? You've been trippin' all day."

"Nothing," James replied coldly.

Michelle was half listening to Jodie and half listening to James and Alexander. "Thanks, Jodie, I'll run it by James and get back to you."

She hung up the telephone and looked across the desk at James. "You feel like celebrating a two-year-old's birthday this evening?"

James would rather spend his Friday evening the way

he always did—in Michelle's den watching a football game with her asleep in his arms. "Whatever you wanna do, Mickey, I don't care."

He was highly upset. Michelle knew it, and so did Alexander. Alexander saw the way Michelle was looking at his friend and knew that she wanted to question him about his mood. He excused himself from Michelle's office. "Uh, I'm gonna go to the bathroom."

When Alexander closed the door behind him, Michelle saw that James had his eyes fixed on something across the office. "You wanna talk about it?," she asked.

"What's to talk about?" he shrugged.

"Whatever's got you in this funky mood."

He looked at her. "Mickey, I'm sorry. I was extremely late for work this morning and don't understand how."

"You overslept?"

"I over, overslept. I missed roll call."

"On the phone last night, you said that you were tired. It's normal to oversleep every now and then."

"It's not just that. I feel kinda out of it. Like the day is passing me by and I can't catch up to it."

"Well, you have been putting in a lot of hours lately. Why don't you cut back?"

"Maybe you're right. I haven't been getting enough sleep."

"When was your last physical? Maybe it's time for a checkup."

"It's been a while since I've seen my doctor. On Monday morning, I'll make an appointment."

"Are you and Alex done for the day?"

James leaned back in his chair and unbuttoned his top button. "Yeah, we're on our way home."

"When you get home, take two aspirin and go to bed. Call me in the morning."

"What are you going to do tonight?"

"Well, that was Jodie who called. She invited us to Mya's birthday party, so I'll stop by there for a few hours."

"I'll go with you."

Michelle loved spending time with James, but he was fatigued. She could see the tiredness in his face. "James, you need to rest."

"I wanna be with you."

Alexander knocked and poked his head in. "You ready, partner?"

"You go ahead, Alex. I'm hanging with my baby tonight."

"Alright, partner. See you on Monday morning. Have a good weekend, Michelle."

He shut Michelle's office door and headed for the elevator. As he waited for the doors to open, Amaryllis walked past him on her way to her desk.

"It was nice meeting you, Amyrella."

She stopped dead in her tracks then turned to look at him. If it was something Amaryllis hated, it was having her name mispronounced or misspelled. As she made her point, her neck danced. "It's Amaryllis; A-m-a-r-y-l-l-i-s. Write it down and make a note of it, okay? And for future reference, if you can't remember how to pronounce my name right, I suggest you ask before you just let anything come out of your mouth." She turned and walked to her desk and sat down.

The elevator doors opened and Alexander stepped onto it. "I'm sorry, I didn't mean to offend you. I think you have a beautiful name"

Amaryllis looked at him like he was being a nuisance. "Why are you still here?"

On that note, Alexander pressed the DOWN button and the elevator doors closed.

Amaryllis realized that Alexander had left solo. That

meant that James was still behind closed doors with Michelle. She went to Michelle's door, pressed her ear against it and heard laughter.

"Oh, I almost forgot, I gotta show you this beautiful card that you and I got in the mail today," Michelle said.

"You and I as in us?"

"Yep, it was delivered here by priority mail. I'll read it to you." Michelle showed James the front of the yellow card decorated with white lace.

"Very pretty, who's it from?" he asked.

"I'll read it and then you tell me who you think sent it, okay?"

"Okay."

"The card reads as follows: *Dear James and Michelle, you don't know me, but my mommy has told me all about you. She said you both were kind, considerate, selfless and most of all, you are Christians. She said that a lot of the attributes she sees in her parents, she also sees them in both of you. She told me that Miss Michelle has played a very important part in making sure that God answered my parents' prayers by sacrificing her favorite thing: chocolate. Mommy says that not only are Miss Michelle and Mr. James good people, they're also good friends to have, and my daddy totally agrees with her. So, I have a very important question to ask the both of you. Think about it, because it's really, really, really important. Will you be my godparents? I love you already, Baby Burton.*"

Michelle looked at James who was mesmerized. "Well, do you know who the card is from?"

"Wow, Mickey, I'm blown away. Yeah, I know who it's from. Chantal and Michael's little bun in the oven."

"Yep, you guessed it. The little bun wants an answer. So, what's it gonna be? Do we accept?"

James smiled. "Are you kidding? How can we turn down this awesome responsibility? Of course, we accept."

"Oh, James, I'm so happy you want this. I was praying you'd feel this way."

"This will be good training for when God blesses us with our own little bun in the oven."

"Honey, I can't wait to become pregnant with your child. Just the thought of walking around with a part of you inside of me is exciting. Even when we're apart, I'll still have you with me."

"You know what, Mickey? Having you in my life confirms that God is alive, real and in control of everything. And I know that He's got favor on my life, because I've done some sinful things back in the day, but to know that He's forgiven me and blessed me with you, puts joy in my spirit. I'm so happy that He allowed one of His angels in eternity to be made into flesh form and brought her into my life to become my wife."

Listening outside of the door, Amaryllis wanted to scream. James was supposed to be saying these words to her, not Michelle. Why should her sister have all the good things in life? Michelle had her own business, her own house, plenty of money, beauty and brains, plus she was Daddy's favorite. And to top it off, she had a man who practically worshipped her. It wasn't fair.

Back inside Michelle's office, Michelle stood and walked around the desk and sat in James' lap. "Wow. What beautiful words."

James saw tears streaming down her face. "Don't get mushy on me. You know I can't handle that."

"I'm sorry, baby, I can't help it. I didn't know that love could be this wonderful. When you first approached me that night at church, love was written all over your face.

And at that exact moment, I knew you were mine. I knew God couldn't be so cruel that He'd allow you to walk into my life then walk out of it. Many nights, I dreamed of our future. We'd be sitting in a park, having a picnic or walking hand in hand on the beach or sitting in a restaurant staring into each other's eyes over a candlelight dinner. God hasn't created a word that expresses how much I love and adore you, James."

"I thank you for courting me the way God commanded you to. I really wanted to wait for my wedding night to give my husband my special gift and often, I prayed for a man who's loving, kind and patient, and look who I got. Not one time has sex been an issue with you and I'm so grateful for that. It's your obedience to God that causes my happiness."

Michelle wiped tears from her eyes. "I'm going to tell you something that you probably don't know." She placed James' open palm on the center of her chest and looked into his eyes. "You literally hold my heart in the palm of your hand." James' face was just as wet as Michelle's and she mocked him. "Don't get mushy on me. You know I can't handle that."

"I'm outdone, Mickey. I don't know what to say behind that."

"Isn't it good to know that we were made for each other?"

James stood up and brought Michelle to a standing position with him; then he held her hands, bowed his head and closed his eyes. "Father God, James and Michelle here. We thank you for what you've done for us. We bless your Holy name, Lord, and we honor your presence in our lives. For as long as we live, Lord, we'll never be able to thank you enough for your loving kindness. And we pray, Lord, that as we embark on the next phase of our lives as husband and wife, that you will continue to keep your arms of grace and mercy all around us. We praise you, Lord, and we worship you. We thank you for your Holy Spirit that's constantly guiding our footsteps. We love you and we reverence your name."

Hearing James' prayer ticked off Amaryllis so much that she didn't know what to do. She walked back over to her desk and felt like tipping it over. She looked at the clock on the wall that read five-fifty P.M. The clerk said the pictures and puzzle would be ready at six o'clock. She grabbed her purse and keys, then walked to the elevator. She turned around and looked at Michelle's closed door. "Pray all you want. I got something for y'all."

When Amaryllis got home from the Photo Mart, she went directly upstairs to her bedroom and locked herself inside. She sat on the bed and opened the package. The two photos of her and James were very clear. She looked at a photograph of James lying naked on his living room sofa with his eyes closed and his hands caressing the breasts of a naked light skinned woman with long blond hair who straddled him. Her back was to the camera, but James's face was fully exposed. The second photograph was of James in the same position with his eyes closed, but the woman was leaning forward. In this photo it wasn't clear whether they were kissing or talking to one another.

Amaryllis unwrapped another package that revealed the first photo made into an eight by ten puzzle. She took the seven-piece puzzle apart, then started to put it back together again. Amaryllis decided to anonymously send one piece per week to Michelle leading up to her wedding. The very last piece of the puzzle would be mailed to Michelle two weeks before she was to walk down the center aisle. Amaryllis brought the last piece of the puzzle to her lips and kissed it. She looked at it and smiled at James' face. Since she hadn't been able to steal him away from Michelle, Amaryllis became angry with him and decided to ruin his life. A picture is worth a thousand words, Amaryllis wondered how many words James would come up with to get out of this mess she was about to place him in.

Chapter 10

The first piece of the puzzle arrived on a Thursday evening at Michelle's town home. Coming from work, Michelle and Amaryllis were entering the living room after getting the mail from the mailbox. Michelle threw her purse on the sofa and kicked off her heels as she glanced through the mail. Amaryllis walked into the kitchen and pretended to get something to drink while watching her sister do her sorting.

When Michelle recognized a bill, she'd put it at the back of the pile. "Bill, bill, junk mail, bill, ooh, a check, junk mail, bill, bill."

The ninth envelope stopped Michelle's flow. She looked at a white letter-sized envelope with her name and address written in calligraphy and in gold ink. There was no return address, so Michelle wondered who it could be from. Amaryllis watched as Michelle tore open the envelope and pulled out a sheet of paper. Enfolded in the paper was a piece to a puzzle that showed someone's feet.

Michelle frowned at what she saw, then read what was typed on the paper.

You like to drink Kool-Aid
I like to drink wine
Here's the first piece to a puzzle
That will surely blow your mind

Michelle frowned and studied the puzzle piece. Why would someone send her a picture of feet?

Amaryllis walked into the living room and asked, "What are you frowning at?"

Michelle gave her the letter and puzzle piece. "Look at this."

Amaryllis didn't have to read it to know what it said, but she did it to humor Michelle.

"Girl, what's this?"

"I don't know. It came in the mail today."

"Where's the rest of the puzzle?"

"Only one piece was in the letter."

Amaryllis looked at the puzzle piece of James' feet. "Don't worry about it. It's probably just someone playing games."

Michelle took the letter and the puzzle piece from Amaryllis. "Yeah, you're probably right." She put the letter and the puzzle piece in the envelope and took it upstairs to her bedroom.

Amaryllis was grinning from ear to ear. It was a game alright. A game that Michelle wouldn't win.

A week and a day later, the mailman brought the office mail to Amaryllis' desk. She saw the gold lettering on an envelope and smiled. There was also a box from Blessed

Events Consulting, addressed to Michelle. Amaryllis wondered which of the two she'd give to her sister first. Michelle was excited about the wedding invitations and would probably tear the box open before opening any other mail. Amaryllis placed the envelope with the gold lettering in Michelle's mail basket on her desk and she placed the box of invitations in the center of the desk. Michelle was off at court and if she was having a good day in the courtroom, as she always did, those new findings would definitely destroy her mood.

At three-thirty P.M., Michelle exited the elevator. "Hey, sis, how are you?"

Amaryllis stopped typing and looked at her. "You're in a great mood."

"Yes, I am, and it's because Price & Associates won the Henderson case today. Life can't possibly get any better than it is right now. Everything is absolutely perfect. If God never did anything else for me for as long as I live, what He's done already is more than enough."

"Good for you, Michelle. I wish I had your attitude," Amaryllis said, knowing that Michelle's carefree mind-set was about to do a three-hundred-sixty-degree turn.

"Get to know God and you can have it."

"Whatever," Amaryllis replied disrespectfully. Michelle was always throwing God in her face. *'You really need to be in church, Amaryllis.' 'You need to get saved, Amaryllis.' 'You should ask God to bless your food before you eat, Amaryllis.' 'Come to church with me and James, Amaryllis.'*

"Has a gorgeous minister called today?"

"Nope. But there's a surprise waiting for you on your desk."

Michelle smiled. "He sent roses, didn't he?"

"Why don't you take a look?"

Michelle walked into her office and saw the big blue box and shouted with joy. "Yay, my wedding invitations are here." She anxiously opened the box and pulled out a single invitation. Suddenly, her grin turned upside down and she hollered out. "Oh, my goodness. What is this? How could this happen?"

Surprise, surprise, surprise. Amaryllis was at her desk with the same silly smile as Gomer Pyle often wore on television. She composed herself then jumped up and ran into Michelle's office. "Michelle, what's wrong?" Amaryllis played the role of a devoted sister, ready to do combat with whatever was ailing Michelle. Michelle was stunned at what she was reading, and couldn't say anything. Amaryllis walked over to her and asked again. "What's wrong?"

Tears were streaming down Michelle's face. "My invitations are ruined."

Amaryllis took the invitation from her hand and read it. "How in the world could they mess this up?"

"The question is why is your name on there at all, Amaryllis?" Michelle wasn't the least bit suspicious that her baby sister was the culprit.

"Sweetie, sometimes these things happen."

"How?"

"Since I was the one who actually placed the order, maybe the lady just got the names mixed up."

"Well, I'm gonna find out." Michelle snatched up her telephone and was getting ready to dial when Amaryllis stopped her.

"Michelle, you are in no mood to talk to anyone. Let me handle this for you. Besides, you're too nice. When I get through with this company, they won't know what hit them."

Amaryllis took the telephone from Michelle and told

her to dial the number. After a couple of rings, someone answered. "Yes, who am I speaking with? Yolanda, this is Michelle Price and I've just received my wedding invitations. Heck no, I'm not pleased with them. Because you screwed up the entire order, that's why. No, that's not what I faxed you. Hold on a minute."

She motioned for Michelle to get the copy from her file cabinet. Michelle gave Amaryllis the manila envelope. "Yolanda, I'm holding in my hand what my secretary faxed you. I told you, what? Listen, Yolanda, my wedding is less than seven weeks away. I want this order corrected and sent to me within the next three days. And if your company can't get a simple name right, then maybe you shouldn't be in business. And just so you know, I sue companies that try to get over on people. You've got three days . . . Yes, that's fine."

Amaryllis hung up the telephone and looked at Michelle. "See, problem solved. Your new and corrected invitations will be here in three days, and Yolanda's gonna eat the bill. You'll be receiving a refund check."

Michelle looked at her sister in awe. "I'm so glad you're on my team. I thought you were gonna get ghetto on her."

"If you weren't sitting here, I would have. But since you won't let me cuss, you missed out."

Amaryllis picked up the box of wedding invitations. "I'm sure you don't wanna look at these anymore, so I'll shred them."

"Thanks, sis, and please don't mention this incident to James."

Amaryllis closed Michelle's door behind her and headed into the file room to shred the invitations. She had thought about keeping one invitation for a souvenir but decided against it. Michelle was upset and Amaryllis found satisfaction in that. James, on the other hand, was destined to pay a bigger price.

Michelle reached for the mail in her basket. She saw the gold calligraphy lettering on an envelope and paused. She slowly opened the letter and saw another puzzle piece enclosed in a sheet of paper. This piece showed a part of a gray leather sofa and the left side of a light skinned person's back and butt. She read the letter.

Roses are red
Violets are blue
This world is full of surprises
There's one waiting just for you

After shredding the invitations, Amaryllis came back into Michelle's office. "It's quitting time, Michelle."

She saw Michelle sitting at her desk with one hand over her mouth. With the other she was holding the puzzle piece. Amaryllis walked further into her office. "Another letter?"

"Amaryllis, I think someone's stalking me."

Amaryllis read the letter and looked at the puzzle piece. "Don't get upset. Let's take it home and put it with the other one and see what we've got."

Once at home, they connected the two pieces. It was clear that a naked light skinned woman was straddling a man.

"Who in the world is sending this to me?," Michelle asked Amaryllis.

"Michelle, it's probably a bridesmaid joke."

Michelle thought about that. "You know what, Amaryllis? Jodie *is* the type to do something this crazy."

"See, it's nothing for you to worry about." *For now.*

* * *

On Saturday morning, Michelle had just finished vacuuming the entire town home when the telephone rang. "Hello?"

"Hi, Michelle, this is Tamara Brown from One Magnificent Moment. Your wedding gown has arrived along with your maid of honor, bridesmaid and flower girl dresses."

Michelle was very excited. After yesterday's issue with the wedding invitations, she could use some good news. "That's wonderful, Tamara."

"When would you and your ladies like to come in for your fittings?"

"How about today?" Michelle squealed.

"Fine, I'll make an appointment for one o'clock this afternoon," Tamara said.

"Great, that gives me plenty of time to round everyone up."

Michelle hurried upstairs and knocked on Amaryllis' door, then poked her head in. "Good morning, sis."

Amaryllis was lying on the bed watching television in her usual funky mood. "What's so good about it?"

"The bridal boutique just called. Our dresses are in and we have a one o'clock appointment for a fitting."

Amaryllis didn't respond to Michelle's exciting news. She kept her focus on the television.

"Amaryllis, did you hear me?"

"Yeah," she answered nonchalantly.

"Aren't you excited?"

Excited for what? It's not my wedding. Amaryllis hopped out of bed and went into the bathroom. "Of course, I am. I'm hungry; can you make me cinnamon toast?"

"No, I'm gonna treat my ladies to breakfast at the Pancake House before the fitting, so get ready."

Michelle went downstairs to her bedroom and called Jodie. "Good morning, Jodie, what are you up to?"

"Hey, girl, I'm making oatmeal for Mya. This little girl acts like she's a maniac. No one can say two words to her until she gets at least three tablespoons of this stuff in her belly."

"Well, let her throw a tantrum just a little bit longer. I'll be there in an hour to take you two to breakfast, then we're going to the bridal boutique to try on our dresses."

"The dresses are in? Ooh, I'm so excited."

"I'm glad someone is." Michelle was upset that her sister hadn't shared in her joy.

"What do you mean?"

"When I told Amaryllis, she behaved as though she couldn't care less."

"So. Don't let that bring you down. This is all about you, Michelle," Jodie encouraged.

"I know, Jodie, but she's my sister."

"Like I said. So?"

"You don't understand."

"No, Michelle, *you* don't understand. You're preparing to marry a man who worships the husk on your feet."

"I ain't gat no husk on my feet."

"Umph, umph, umph. Did you hear yourself, Michelle? You said, 'I ain't gat no.' Aren't you a college graduate? You know better than that, Counselor."

"Whatever. I still ain't gat no husk on my feet."

"And she says it again. Anyway, back to your sister. This is supposed to be the happiest time in *your* life. You don't have time to pacify anyone who can't get behind you and support your mood. And I don't like your sister's attitude. I only met Amaryllis twice when I came to visit you at the law firm. Her attitude was very chilly both times.

Even when I call your house, if she answers she's not cordial at all. Whenever I ask to speak to you, I hear a thump, like she throws the receiver. Amaryllis acts as though the whole world revolves around her, and I think she's jealous of you."

"Jealous, of what?"

"Of your life and what you and James have."

Michelle refused to believe that. "Jodie, that's crazy. Amaryllis is my sister and I'll share whatever I have with her and she knows that."

"Michelle, sisters share their parents, clothes and secrets, not their men. Do you feel me, girl?"

"What are you saying, that Amaryllis wants to be me?"

"Uh, yeeaah. And you should keep your eyes and ears open where James is concerned. The man cherishes and adores you and he lets the whole world know it. A lot of women see that and want a man like yours for themselves. But there's only one James Bradley and you got him. If a woman can't get her own perfect man, what's to stop her from trying to get someone else's?"

"Girl, you're starting to sound like my father."

"Doesn't that tell you something?"

"Amaryllis is my flesh and blood. I can't imagine her betraying me."

"Humph, like Cain and Abel? Listen, Michelle, I know you love your sister and you're not supposed to imagine things like that, but that's where I come in as your best friend. I'm just looking out for you, that's all."

"I trust James."

"And you should because he's trustworthy. But we're not talking about James. It's Amaryllis you need to be asking yourself if you can trust."

Chapter 11

After eating their share of pancakes, Michelle and her ladies arrived at One Magnificent Moment at a quarter 'til one. She signed her name in the registry, and five minutes later, a lady approached her.

"Hi, Michelle; I'm Tamara."

Michelle smiled. "Hi, Tamara. These are my ladies. My sister, Amaryllis, is my maid of honor, my best friend, Jodie, is my bridesmaid, and this little cutie is Mya, my flower girl."

Tamara gave them a huge grin. "It's nice to meet all of you. I have your gowns all set up for you. Follow me, please."

Jodie grabbed Mya by the hand and the women followed Tamara to a room where their dresses were hanging and looking beautiful. The first thing Michelle saw was her wedding gown and she squealed with delight. "It's so beautiful."

They wanted to save the best dress for last, so Michelle helped Mya into her dress as Amaryllis and Jodie tried on their own dresses. Mya jumped and twisted in the white lace and chiffon as she admired herself in the mirror. Michelle sat with tears in her eyes as she looked at her ladies in their gowns.

Amaryllis wasn't in a festive mood, but she did have to admit that the burnt orange Donatella Versace gowns that Michelle selected for her and Jodie were beautiful. Except for the need for a four-inch hem, their gowns fit them perfectly. Jodie was properly measured at the bridal boutique three months ago and because Amaryllis was still in Chicago at the time of the initial fitting, she had given her measurements to Tamara over the phone. They brought their stilettos with them and the gowns were still too long. Mya's dress was perfect, but when the time came for her to take it off, she had a fit. In the dress, she looked like a little princess and she knew it.

Michelle had even bought Mya a miniature tiara to match the one she was wearing herself. Michelle lifted the crown from Mya's head and she fell out and started rolling, kicking and screaming. She still had her dress on, so Michelle quickly picked her up. "You can't keep the crown on, Myaboo." Michelle said. She sat Mya down on her lap and tried to unzip the back of the dress. Mya slouched down, then fell to the floor. Michelle looked at her mother. "Jodie, take this dress off of her."

Jodie was busy getting out of her own dress. "Nope. You're always sayin' you want a house full of kids. Consider yourself in training." Jodie turned her back to Michelle and continued undressing.

Michelle got on her knees and literally fought with Mya to get the dress off. When she finally pulled the dress over Mya's head, Michelle was out of breath. She sat on the floor and watched Mya throw a temper tantrum. Tamara knocked on the door and asked what all the fuss was about and Michelle explained that the little princess wanted to remain in her fairytale dress.

Mya got up from the floor and snatched the tiara from Michelle's hand and put it back on her head. Michelle took it off and Mya fell down again kicking and screaming. The kicking isn't what got to Michelle, but it was the piercing scream that was driving her nuts. She asked Tamara for the price of the small tiara.

"That particular style costs eighty-nine dollars," Tamara answered.

"Can you please put in a rush order for another one?" Michelle set the tiara on top of Mya's head and she immediately stopped screaming. She decided to let Mya take that tiara home with her. Michelle figured she'd do the smart thing and order another one because by the time the wedding date arrived, the tiara Mya currently had on her head would be destroyed.

Mya stood in front of the mirror and started twisting and jumping again. She didn't even care that every time she jumped, snot dripped from her nose.

Michelle looked at Jodie. "You do this everyday, huh?"

"Everyday, all day; so as Bishop T.D. Jakes says, 'Get ready, get ready, get ready.' "

Michelle placed the back of her hand on her forehead. "I don't know, I may have to rethink some things."

"You're a preacher's wife now, Michelle. You've got to set that great example."

"What example?"

Jodie chuckled. "To be fruitful and multiply."

"I did say that I wanted a house full, didn't I?"

"I believe those were your exact words."

Michelle looked at Mya bending and chewing on the eighty-nine dollar tiara. "Lord, help me."

With Mya satisfied and quiet, it was time for Michelle to

try on her gown. Both Jodie and Amaryllis helped her. Between the two of them, it took twenty whole minutes to tie the strings of the corset on the Reem Acra couture white gown. They attached her train and put the tiara on her head, along with the veil, and stood back to admire her. Michelle was beautiful anyway, but the white gown accentuated her chocolate brown skin. With the dress fitting her every curve, sparkling at every turn she made, and the diamond crown on her head, Michelle was every bit a queen.

Mya walked up to Michelle. "Ooh, pwittee."

Dressed in the strapless gown, Michelle looked at herself in the mirror. "It feels a little snug around my breasts."

Amaryllis spoke. "That's because you're cursed like me with those double D's."

"They are not a curse, they're a blessing," Jodie said.

Michelle chuckled. "In what way, Jodie?"

"Sweet innocent, Michelle, must I teach you everything? We're gonna buy you a push up bra and stuff those coconuts in it. While you're walking down the aisle toward James, your cleavage will be wiggling and bouncing, and that, my virgin friend, will cause James to lose his mind."

Michelle and Jodie laughed, but Amaryllis found no humor in it at all.

"I don't wanna look trashy, Jodie," Michelle said.

"Not trashy, Michelle, but sexy is more like it. Remember how James acted a year ago when you came to church that night y'all met? You were looking as fine as you wanted to look and that messed him up. You had on a simple spaghetti strap dress. Imagine what it will do to him if you showed a little cleavage. Girl, he'll probably tell Bishop Graham to skip the vows and go right to the 'I do's'. Then he'll pick you up and carry you to the limousine and go straight to the hotel for a quickie before the reception. You've had James on lock down for a year and you know he's set on go."

The two of them laughed again. "Jodie, you are a bad, bad girl," Michelle said.

"And in six more weeks, you will be one too."

After they had left the bridal boutique, Michelle stopped at J.C. Penney to find a bustier that would make James' knees crumble.

"You're rubbing off on me, Jodie," Michelle said as Jodie helped her into a hundred dollar strapless bustier.

"That's a good thang, girlfriend."

Amaryllis didn't want to be a part of Michelle's venture to buy undergarments that would make James' head spin. She faked a headache and sat in Michelle's truck and babysat Mya while the child napped.

Michelle and Jodie returned to the SUV. The ladies were on their way to Jodie's house when Michelle's cellular phone rang. She looked at the caller I.D. and recognized James' number. "Hello, gorgeous. Not me, you are."

Amaryllis' blood began to boil.

"The girls and I just left the bridal boutique for our fittings. My dress is beautiful. You're gonna love it."

Jodie was sitting behind Michelle. She leaned closer behind the driver's seat and spoke loud enough for James to hear. "You're gonna explode."

Michelle waved her hand, motioning for Jodie to be quiet. "Uh, she didn't say anything, baby."

Jodie yelled again. "I hope you're a patient man, James."

Michelle waved her hand at Jodie again. "Uh, she said don't forget our plans, James. Remember, tonight we're going out to dinner with her and Michael. Afterward, we're going to see the stage play, *Men Cry In The Dark.*"

* * *

Amaryllis and Michelle got home at four-thirty P.M. Michelle had gotten the mail from the mailbox and saw the gold writing on an envelope. In the living room, Michelle set her purse, bags and keys on the cocktail table. "Jodie sent another one, Amaryllis."

The puzzle piece showed the other half of a woman's back and butt, and the man's legs and thighs.

"I hope she's not sending me a picture of her and Michael while they're in the heat of the moment," Michelle chuckled as she read the letter.

> *Nicholas Price has a little lamb*
> *Whose fleece is as white as snow*
> *Michelle is her name*
> *Purity is her game*
> *Being churchy is all she knows*

Michelle folded the letter and took it and the puzzle piece up to her room. "That Jodie is crazy."

Amaryllis stood in the living room thinking to herself, *Three puzzle pieces down and four to go.*

James rang Michelle's bell an hour early. She opened the door dressed in her red, satin robe. "Sweetie, you're early."

James looked at his bride to be. Even in her robe, wearing no make-up and with her hair pulled back into a ponytail, Michelle was breathtaking. "I know, baby, but I've been waiting to see you all day. I couldn't stay away any longer."

"That is so sweet, James. You always know just the right thing to say. You're good for my ego." She pulled him inside and hugged him, neither of them realizing that Amaryllis was at the top of the stairs listening.

"I'm going upstairs to take a shower. Why don't you go into the den and watch television?"

"Okay, baby. I think a game might be on."

As Michelle turned to walk away, James pulled her back to him. He started the kiss that followed, but it was Michelle that deepened it. When their lips parted, James was breathless.

"You trying to test me, Mickey? You better go on upstairs with that or else."

"Or else what?"

"Or else I'll backslide and it'll be your fault."

Michelle double dared James. She kept standing there, tracing his lips with her index finger. "I don't think you got it in you, preacher."

James reached for Michelle again and she took off screaming and running toward the stairs. Amaryllis hurried into her bedroom on the third floor.

James chased Michelle halfway up to her bedroom, but before he could reach the top step, Michelle slammed her door shut and locked him out. James, laughing, walked back downstairs and got himself a glass of Kool-Aid. He took it into the den and sat down to watch television while he waited on Michelle. Amaryllis stood outside of Michelle's door and made sure she heard the water from the shower before she went downstairs.

James was into the television when Amaryllis came and stood nude in front of it. "Is this what you want?"

James was in shock. He looked at Amaryllis' body and had no doubt that it was just as built and beautiful as Michelle's. Alexander was right, they were identical in every way. But it was Michelle's body that he'd been waiting a whole year for, and he'd continue to wait until the night of their wedding.

He took his gaze away from Amaryllis' pierced navel and looked into her eyes. "Not from you."

"Did you really think Michelle was gonna let you have her?"

"Let me tell you something, Amaryllis. I could have caught Mickey going up those steps if I really wanted to. I let her get away because I knew she was only fooling around. I respect my woman and I'm willing to wait until she's ready. Besides, there is nothing you can do for me. Mickey is all the woman I need."

Amaryllis walked to James and straddled him. He pushed her off and jumped up. "Get off of me, girl. When Mickey comes down, I'm telling her what you're doing."

Amaryllis gave James a wicked smile. "I dare you." She turned and slowly sashayed toward the stairs. A moment later, she looked over her shoulder and caught James admiring her.

James sat down on the sofa and exhaled loudly. At that moment he realized the devil truly hated him.

Chapter 12

In the sanctuary after church, Cookie hugged Michelle. "It's almost that time. How much longer until the big day?"

Michelle squealed in delight. "A little over a month. We've been planning this wedding for months and now I'm getting nervous."

"It's natural to be a little nervous."

Michelle's expression became serious. "Can I ask you a personal question, First Lady?"

"Of course, sweetie."

Michelle looked around to make sure they were out of everyone's hearing range and whispered, "Were you a virgin on your wedding night?"

Cookie chuckled. "I knew that was the question."

"The reason I asked is because James will be my first and I'm freaking out. My nervousness isn't about the wedding. I'm nervous about that night. I don't know how to talk to him or how to touch him. I don't know if I should wear a long sheer nightgown or something short, made of leather that comes with a whip and handcuffs. Do I initiate the lovemaking or let James take control?"

As Michelle was speaking, Cookie could see her hands shaking. She grabbed Michelle's hands and guided her to the first pew and sat down. "I understand how you feel. I won't say that you won't be nervous because every bride is; *especially* a virgin. And yes, I was a virgin on my wedding night and my husband knew it. Does James know that you're pure?"

"Yes."

"James is like a son to me and I happen to know that he's a very loving and caring man. My advice to you is let him be king. In other words, relax, follow his lead and go with the flow. Allow him to explore your body and mark every area with his scent. I have no clue if James is a virgin or not, but if he is, he will be just as nervous as you."

"He's not a virgin, Cookie."

"And how do you feel about that?"

Michelle shrugged her shoulders. "To be honest with you, Cookie, I don't feel one way or another. Truth be told, I was shocked when James revealed his sexual past to me, but I have no control over what he did before he and I met. I'm just thankful that he hasn't pressured me for sex. He's been very patient.

"Well, if that's the case, then he's gonna want to make up for what he hasn't been getting in a long time."

"What does that mean?"

"It means you can leave the whip and leather in the store. But if you come out of the bathroom and see James lying on the bed wearing a Lone Ranger mask and a red silk thong, then you've got yourself an undercover freak."

Michelle hollered out loud then covered her mouth when she attracted attention. "What do you know about being a freak, First Lady?"

"You're looking at one," Cookie answered with no shame. Michelle hollered out again. "Oh, no. I don't believe it."

"Believe it, honey. I may be a pastor's wife, but I'm a woman first. And every move my husband throws my way, I can match it or master it. Why do you think we were late for church this morning?"

Michelle's dark cheeks turned crimson red and she lowered her voice. "On a Sunday, Cookie?"

"Girl, yeah. On a Monday, Tuesday, Wednesday, Thursday, Friday and twice on Saturdays if I make him pancakes."

Michelle laughed so loud that she caught James' attention.

He walked over to them. "What in the world has got you waking up the dead?" he asked his fiancé.

Cookie looked at him. "What's your favorite breakfast food, James?"

"I'm coo-coo for Cocoa Puffs."

They laughed at him as Cookie looked at Michelle. "Girl, if I were you, I'd buy stock in Cocoa Puffs."

The women were hysterical. James stood looking foolish because he knew that he was the center of a private joke between his First Lady and future wife. "Uh, Mickey, I'll wait for you in the car," James said as he turned to leave. When James walked away, he heard laughter and turned around and saw them looking at him.

Cookie grabbed Michelle's hands and held them inside her own. "With all kidding aside, Michelle, I want you to know that lovemaking with your husband will be wonderful. I'm sure on the first night James will take control, because he knows you're delicate. But there are gonna be times when he'll want you to initiate intimacy and that's fine. During this time with him, you're allowed to let your guard down and be open and carefree. Hold nothing back from James. His body is yours and your body is his. The marriage bed is undefiled. In other words, what goes on in your bedroom is between you and your husband, and as long as you're not hurting one another physically, enjoy that private time. Your main goal, as James' wife, is to keep him happy, satisfied and *at home*.

"Never, ever; I'll say it four times, 'Never, ever, ever, ever' make the mistake of denying James access to what's his. If you have a headache, take two aspirin, cast the pain out in the name of Jesus, then pleasure your husband and . . . wear . . . him . . . out. I want you to really understand what I'm saying to you, Michelle. You know what you got in James. He is a good man and there are plenty of women who would love to have your blessing.

"And trust me on this, sweet baby, whatever you do on your wedding night that pleases James, is what you gotta keep doing throughout your marriage to *keep* James. One more thing, if it turns out that James *is* a freak, then you've got to become a freak too because it takes one to keep one. Don't you dare become so holy that you limit yourself between the sheets with your husband, because what you won't do, another woman most certainly will. So, get on top of your game and let James turn you every which way but loose. I guess what I'm really trying to say is . . . drop it like it's hot."

On the following Wednesday evening, Michelle held a fourth envelope in her hands addressed to her in gold lettering. The puzzle piece showed the left shoulder of the woman with blond hair.

> *Virgins are sheltered*
> *And they never get none*
> *But as you can see in this picture*
> *Blondes do have more fun*

Upstairs in her bedroom, Michelle added the piece to the puzzle and thought to herself. *So, Jodie is wearing a wig. I always knew she was a freak.*

As Michelle was going downstairs, Amaryllis was coming upstairs. She saw a blue box from Blessed Events Consulting in Michelle's hand and asked, "Where are you going?"

"Over to James' to address these invitations. I gotta mail them in the morning. You wanna come with me?"

"No, there's an eight o'clock movie coming on that I wanna see."

"Okay, I may be late getting in, so don't wait up."

Late? What does that mean? "You're not spending the night with him, are you?" Amaryllis asked Michelle the question like she was scolding a ten year old.

"Excuse me?"

"How late are you going to be?"

Michelle was stunned at her sister's tone of voice. "I don't know, and why is that your business?"

Amaryllis knew she had to back off of Michelle. She didn't want Michelle to know that her going to James' house infuriated her. "Girl, I'm just trippin'. Don't pay me any attention."

Amaryllis went upstairs to her bedroom and slammed the door. Michelle wanted to go up and talk to her, but decided to let it go. She remembered what Jodie said about people not being happy for her and James. Amaryllis was too old to be behaving that way and Michelle was too old to be worried about it.

In her bedroom, Amaryllis placed a stamp on another letter addressed to Michelle and put it in her purse. She'd mail it in the morning.

James greeted Michelle with a hug and kiss when she arrived at his place. "Hi, gorgeous."

"You're the gorgeous one," Michelle insisted.

"Not me, you are."

"No, you are."

Michelle sat down on the sofa. She leaned back and something dawned on her. She looked at the gray leather sofa and recalled seeing it somewhere other than in James' living room. *The puzzle*, she thought to herself.

Chapter 13

The following Friday evening, James, with his best man, Alexander, his groomsman, Michael, and his future father in-law, Nicholas, all looked like royalty as they modeled their white tuxedos and white patent leather shoes at Just The Right Tux. James spotted a white top hat and a cane on a nearby rack. He put the hat on his head and then leaned on the cane, crossing his right ankle over his left. "Well, gentlemen, how do I look?"

Michael couldn't help himself. "All you need is a pair of bifocals and you could pass for a black Mr. Peanut."

The men laughed, then Alexander stepped to him and took the hat from his head. "Don't get carried away."

"Jealousy doesn't look good on you guys. Don't be bitter just because I'm about to marry the most beautiful woman God has created," James boasted.

Michael looked at him. "That's impossible, James, because I married that woman four years ago."

"Michael, you're crazy. Jodie ain't even in Mickey's league," James argued.

"What? My wife will give Michelle a run for her money and leave her bankrupt."

From his wallet, James withdrew a picture of Michelle. "Look at how long, silky and shiny my baby's hair is. Look at how pretty her eyes are."

Michael showed a picture of Jodie. "So what? Who cares about hair? Look at how beautiful Jodie's nose and lips are."

"So what? Mickey's color can put Hershey's out of business," James said proudly.

Alexander stepped in. "That's because she eats chocolate so much that it sank down into her pores, with her stingy self."

"And Jodie's hips are the reason hip huggers are back in style," Michael said.

"So what? Mickey's got double D's."

That shut Michael up, and he placed Jodie's picture back in his wallet. "I can't touch that one."

Alexander said, "I would love to take both Michelle and Jodie off your hands, but since they're already spoken for, I'll have to settle for Amaryllis. Now she's finer than fine. How about it, Nick, may I have your daughter's hand in marriage?"

"Alex, I'll pay you to marry her and move to Alaska," Nicholas responded.

"Why Alaska?" Alexander asked.

"Because it's ice cold there and so is Amaryllis' attitude. She'll fit right in."

Alexander chuckled. "I could live with that. We'll settle down and get a penguin for a pet."

James spoke. "Don't be surprised if you come home from work and find that penguin on top of the stove boiling in a pot of water."

* * *

That evening, Michelle opened another letter. This puzzle piece showed the right side of the woman's back and butt. Michelle could also see her holding the man's hands as they cupped her breasts.

When I was a girl I played with dolls
But that was then
Now that I'm a woman
I like to play with men

Michelle connected the piece to the rest of the puzzle. It was clear from what she received so far that Jodie and Michael were having a good time disguising themselves. But the sofa they were on wasn't the sofa that was currently in their living room. Maybe it was an old picture, because in the two years she'd known Jodie and Michael, they'd had a white sofa. Michelle was certain that the sofa in the picture matched James'. Michael and James were friends. Was it possible that he and Jodie were at James' apartment? Michelle quickly dismissed this thought because James would never permit this type of behavior on his sofa.

On Sunday afternoon, after church, Nicholas, Michelle and James were enjoying grilled halibut, scalloped potatoes, buttered string beans, a garden salad and dinner rolls. Amaryllis was invited to church that morning by Michelle but she refused to get out of bed. She told Michelle she had major cramps.

They were at the Marquis Banquet Hall, sampling the reception dinner Michelle and James had chosen for their guests.

"Baby girl, where's Veronica's daughter?" Nicholas asked Michelle.

She looked at her father in shame. "What did I tell you about that, Daddy? Amaryllis is *your* daughter too."

"That's what Veronica told me, but I don't have proof of that."

"The proof is in Amaryllis' face. She looks just like you."

"No, *you* look just like me," Nicholas insisted.

"Well, Amaryllis and I can pass for twins. So, if I look like you and she looks like me, then she looks like you."

Nicholas didn't understand that tongue twister. "What?"

"Never mind, Daddy. I invited Amaryllis to church with us and to get a free meal afterward, but she said she had the cramps from hell."

James thought to himself, *Good for her. She raises hell, she deserves cramps from hell.*

"How did your tuxedo fit?" Michelle asked Nicholas.

"The sleeves were too long, but overall, it fit pretty well."

She turned her attention to James. "And yours, honey?"

James had just put a fork full of food in his mouth and had to wait until he swallowed to speak. "Mine fit perfectly. I wanted to sport a top hat and cane, but Alex and Michael wouldn't let me."

"Remind me to thank them later," Michelle said.

Nicholas looked at Michelle. "Baby Girl, have you been showing James your breasts?" He wore no emotion on his face. It was as though he'd asked Michelle what time of day it was.

James was drinking iced tea and spit it out across the table. Michelle was swallowing string beans and almost choked. She looked at Nicholas in shock. "What?"

"Has James seen your breasts?"

James would have rather been anywhere else other than where he was right then. Michelle looked at him and saw a blank expression on his face. He wouldn't look at her.

"Why would you ask something like that, Daddy?"

"I'm just curious."

"But why?"

"Because I am."

Michelle looked at James as she answered her father's question. "No, James has never seen my breasts."

Just then the host came to the table and spoke to all of them. "Can I get anyone anything else?"

Nicholas looked at James and Michelle. "Is the food okay with you two?"

Michelle had an attitude and didn't speak. James knew she was angry and spoke for the both of them. "Everything was fine. I think we've just confirmed our menu."

Insisting on paying for the reception, Nicholas excused himself and went to the manager's office to take care of the bill.

As soon as her father was out of sight, Michelle threw her napkin onto her plate, leaned back in her chair, looked at James and waited for him to speak. He looked at her and the only thing he could say was, "I'm sorry, Mickey."

"Sorry about what?" she asked sternly.

"For opening my big mouth."

"You told my father that you've seen my breasts?"

"Not exactly."

"What do you mean *not exactly*?"

"See, what had happened was—"

"I don't wanna hear a lie, James. Start over."

James took a deep breath. "Okay, Mickey, we were trying on our tuxes and somehow, Michael and I started comparing you and Jodie. He was saying how good Jodie's hips look, and before I knew it, I commented on the size of your breasts."

Michelle couldn't believe she was hearing this. "What was the comment?"

James knew that if he told her, she'd be furious. "Sweetie, please don't make me repeat it."

She tightened her lips. "What was the comment?"

James paused and took another deep breath. "I told them your breasts' size."

Michelle's eyes grew wide. "You what?"

"Baby, I'm so sorry. It was a stupid thing to do, and I should've known better."

"I can't believe you did this in front of my father."

"Mickey, I'm so sorry."

"Why didn't you tell me about this earlier?"

"Because I didn't think Nick would ask you about it. It was just us men talking."

"Well, thanks a lot for putting me in such an awkward position in front of my father. I appreciate it, James."

"Mickey, sugar baby bubble gum, what can I do to make this up to you?"

"I don't know, *you* tell *me*."

He grabbed her hand. "I'll do anything."

"This is gonna cost you chocolate covered raisins, chocolate kisses and a whole bunch of Chunkys. But you can start by realizing that you are a grown man and what we have is a personal relationship. My body and what we do is not to be discussed with anyone, ever."

James kissed the back of Michelle's hand. "It will never happen again."

At four P.M. Friday, the telephone rang and Amaryllis answered it. "Price & Associates, Amaryllis speaking."

"Hey, it's me, Jodie. What time are you leaving?"

Amaryllis lowered her voice as to not allow Michelle to hear her conversation with Jodie. They were trying to pull off a surprise bachelorette party. "I'll try and get out of here in the next ten minutes."

"Can you stop and pick up the cake for me? I thought I'd have time to get it myself, but I had to get back here and relieve Michael so he can be on time for James' bachelor party tonight."

This was news to Amaryllis. "The boys are giving James a bachelor party tonight?"

"Uh-huh. It's gonna be at Alexander's house."

Thanks for the 411. "Sure, I'll pick up the cake on my way to your house."

"Thanks, Amaryllis. I appreciate it."

No; thank you. She hung up from Jodie and walked into Michelle's office. "I have a headache."

Michelle looked at her. "Amaryllis, you have more headaches than anyone I know. You should see a doctor about that. You want me to kiss it and make it better?"

"No, I'm leaving. I'll see you at home."

"Okay, I won't be too much longer."

For the next two hours, Michelle worked on a case that would have her in court for three days next week. She thought about Amaryllis and was on her way home to see about her until her cellular phone rang. She recognized Jodie's home number. "Hi, Jodie. What's up?"

Jodie was on the other end sounding hysterical. "Michelle, where are you?"

"I'm at the firm, what's wrong?"

She was crying and Michelle was getting nervous. "Jodie, what's wrong?"

"I need you to come to my house."

"What happened?" Michelle asked while grabbing her purse and keys and heading for the door. Jodie disconnected the call without a reply.

Michelle arrived at Jodie's house in less than ten minutes. She rang the doorbell twice, but didn't get an answer. She knocked on the door and it opened a bit. Michelle stepped into the foyer. "Jodie?" The house seemed empty as she walked into the living room. "Jodie?" she called out again.

At once, the lights came on and Michelle heard, "Surprise!"

Before her, stood all the women from her firm, Nicholas' friend, Margaret, three of Michelle's neighbors, a few ladies from the church, her secretary, Chantal, Cookie and Amaryllis. Someone pulled a string and balloons fell from the ceiling. Michelle stood in the middle of the living room with tears in her eyes. "Thank you all so much, but I said that I didn't want a bachelorette party."

Jodie came from behind the crowd and hugged her. "That's why I didn't tell you about it. And thanks for coming to my rescue."

"Girl, you had me driving like a fool trying to get here. I thought something had happened to Michael or Mya. My heart was racing the entire time I was driving."

"I got something that'll calm your nerves. Come on and have a seat." Jodie sat Michelle in a chair in the middle of the living room. The music started and a man built like his name should be Dexter, descended down the stairs wearing a construction worker's uniform.

Michelle saw him and screamed. She covered her eyes with her hands. "No, no, no, Jodie. This can't happen."

Her protests were completely ignored as the ladies hooped and hollered for the dancer to do his thing. He gave Michelle special attention as he danced all around her. He shed his hardhat, tool belt and work pants, then stood in front of her wearing a wife-beater and red silk boxer shorts. Michelle laughed and looked at Cookie.

"It was the closest I thought I should come to red silk thongs, Michelle," Cookie said with a wink.

Jodie had forewarned him that the guest of honor was a church-going woman who was engaged to a minister. She'd asked him to keep his show tasteful. When the song ended, he stood Michelle up, accepted the twenty-dollar bill she tucked into the side waistband of his shorts, kissed her cheek and congratulated her. From the money the women threw at him and what Jodie had paid, he left with almost five hundred dollars.

When the dancer left, the women sat around and laughed while they ate. Michelle walked over to Amaryllis. "So, this is why you left the firm so early. What happened to your headache?"

"It went away when Mr. Fix It came down those steps," Amaryllis replied.

Jodie sliced the cake, made with fresh strawberries and butter cream, and served the women as Michelle opened her gifts. Michelle got everything from a long quilted gown that covered her from neck to toe to edible underwear.

Michelle shrieked. "What am I gonna do with this?"

Someone yelled out, "Don't worry. James will know what to do with it."

The living room was filled with laughter.

Jodie set a three-foot gift-wrapped box in front of Michelle. "This is from James."

Michelle opened it and saw one hundred Hershey's Kisses, fifty Chunky's and a container that held one thousand chocolate covered raisins. Jodie gave her the card he sent with it and Michelle read it aloud.

"My dearest Mickey Mouse . . . To share in your day, I'm sending sweets for my sweet. It won't be long 'til

*we're married, and I'm looking forward to getting a
double dip of your chocolate. Have fun tonight; because
you deserve it. Luv, James."*

All the women oohed and aahed at James' gift and message. No one noticed that Amaryllis had slipped out of
Jodie's back door five minutes earlier.

After she had showered and sprayed herself with
Michelle's perfume, Amaryllis wrapped her nude body in
Michelle's trench coat. She stepped in a pair of Michelle's
black leather stilettos and stuffed the blond wig in the
coat pocket. From Michelle's telephone book on her
nightstand, Amaryllis jotted down Alexander's address on
a piece of paper. On her way to the bachelor party, she
stopped at a costume store and purchased a Mardi Gras
mask that covered her forehead, eyes and nose.

Alexander and James were riding home after a long day
at the precinct. One of the perks of being a homicide detective was that the job title came with a company car
they shared. James was elated when Alexander offered to
do all of the driving.

James noticed that Alexander was taking a different
route. "Where are we going?"

"My place. I wanna show you something," Alexander
responded.

Ten minutes later, they walked into Alexander's house
and James saw Nicholas, Michael, a few men from the
church, two of James' neighbors and four detectives from
his precinct.

Michael was the first to greet James. "What's up, man?"

James looked at everyone standing around the living
room. "I know this ain't what I think it is."

One of his neighbors spoke. "I don't know what you think it is, but it's a stag party."

James looked at Michael. "Why did you let them do this, man?"

"What are you talking about? This was *my* idea," Michael confessed.

"*Your* idea?"

"Yeah, man, loosen up and have some fun."

The men approached James, shook his hand and congratulated him. Eventually, James started to relax and began to mingle. The men sat around, ate and chatted, then the doorbell rang. Alexander opened it and saw a female sporting a blond wig, wearing a mask, a trench coat and high heels. At first, he was puzzled because he hadn't hired a stripper. He didn't want to offend James, but then he thought that maybe one of the other guys had hired her without telling him about it. He smiled and looked at her. "May I help you?"

"Is James Bradley here?"

"Yes, he is."

A disguised Amaryllis brushed past Alexander and stepped into the living room. All eyes turned toward her. She set the boom box she'd brought on top of the cocktail table and pressed the PLAY button. "Do Me Baby" by Prince filled the living room.

Amaryllis sought James out and pulled him by the hand to stand directly in front of her. He nervously looked at Alexander who shrugged his shoulders. Alexander looked at Michael who shrugged his shoulders. Michael looked at Nicholas who shrugged his shoulders. It was clear that the four of them were innocent and had no clue who this dancer was or where she had come from. But all of that would be discussed later. Right now a beautiful woman with a great body was in the middle of Alexander's living room shaking her goods, and at the moment, that was all that mattered.

"Do me, baby, like you've never done before." When Amaryllis shed the trench coat, the men couldn't hold their tongues. They chanted, laughed and encouraged her to continue doing what she was doing. James stood looking at her and couldn't believe this was happening to him. Amaryllis danced around him, touching him every chance she got. Each time Amaryllis touched him in an inappropriate manner, he quickly removed her hand, but didn't stop her show.

Amaryllis was oblivious to all of the money being thrown at her feet. Her main focus was the man she was dancing for. It didn't even matter to Amaryllis that her father was present, watching everything she did. As she sashayed past Nicholas, he noticed a tattoo of a rose on her butt.

When the song ended, Amaryllis grabbed her trench coat from the floor and put it on. She then picked up the cash, grabbed the boom box and walked out the front door without saying a word.

When she closed the door behind her, James looked at everyone present with an angry expression. "Okay, whose idea was that?"

No one said a word. He looked at Michael. "Was it you, Mike?"

Michael shook his head. "Nope, it wasn't me."

James looked at Alexander again. "Alex?"

"Nope," Alexander concluded.

"Nick, did you set this up?"

"Nope, it wasn't me either." Nichols shrugged his shoulders.

James looked around the room. "Will the guilty party speak up?"

No one said anything.

"Well, whoever you are, I just wanna say one thing: Thank you, 'cause she was fine."

All the men let out a loud sigh and started mingling again.

On the night of her bachelorette party, Michelle received one more piece to the puzzle. She could see all of the woman's rear and the man's legs and arms as he caressed the woman's breasts. Michelle saw more of the sofa.

Knock, knock
Who's there?
Wanda
Wanda, who?
Wandaring about this picture, huh?

Michelle was anxious. Something didn't feel right. In her bedroom, she called Jodie. "Where's the last piece to this puzzle?" she asked through the telephone receiver.

"What are you talking about?"

"The picture of you and Michael getting your freak on."

"Did you drink too much punch, Michelle? What are you talking about?"

"For the past month someone's been sending me pieces to a puzzle that shows a man and a woman having sex on a couch."

"What makes you think it's me and Michael?"

"I don't know, I thought you were playing a joke on me or something."

"Michelle, you ought to know that I wouldn't put me and Michael's business out there like that."

Michelle was frustrated. She didn't know what to believe. "I guess you're right, Jodie. But if you're not sending this to me, then who is?"

"I can't answer that."

"I guess I'll have to wait for the last piece. Don't forget that next Thursday night is the wedding rehearsal at the church." She hung up from Jodie and studied the puzzle again. The only piece missing was of the man's face, but Michelle couldn't take her eyes away from the sofa. *Could it be possible? Is he capable? No, it's not possible. James loves me and I know it.*

In court Wednesday afternoon, Michelle was a wreck. She was anticipating the delivery of the last piece to the puzzle. Not only could she not concentrate, but when the time came for her to cross examine the defendant, her mind went blank. She couldn't remember which case she was working on. She searched her briefcase for her notes and found them missing. She silently reprimanded herself for allowing the devil to take over her mind like this.

Needless to say, Michelle lost her first case in almost four years of practicing law. Her perfect record had been shattered. She exited the courtroom with tears in her eyes and ran straight into her father's arms.

"What happened, Baby Girl?"

Michelle was too distraught to explain. "Just get me out of here, Daddy."

Nicholas walked Michelle to her Jaguar. "Talk to me."

Michelle was nervous and shaking. "I don't know what happened. I couldn't concentrate."

"Are you okay to drive to the office?"

"I'm not going back to the office. I'm going home. I'll call you later." Michelle got into her car and drove away.

Michelle got the mail from the mailbox and froze. She stared at the envelope with the gold lettering. She walked into the living room and set all the mail, except one envelope, on the cocktail table. She wanted to open it, but then again, she was afraid. With shaky hands, she tore the envelope open and saw that there was no letter inside with the puzzle piece. Instead, there was a photograph. Slowly she pulled them out and saw what she didn't want to see. She held the puzzle piece of James' face in her hands. In the photograph, James lay on the sofa, nude, with his eyes closed, caressing the breasts of a woman wearing a blonde wig who was straddling him. Michelle clutched her heart and fell to her knees, gasping for air.

Right on cue, Amaryllis descended the stairs. "Michelle, what's wrong?"

She couldn't say anything. She looked at Amaryllis as though she didn't know who she was. Amaryllis saw the puzzle piece and picture in her hand then knelt down and pulled Michelle into her arms. "Sis, I'm so sorry. How could he do this to you? I knew he was no good for you. James tried to come on to me a few times, but I didn't want to tell you because I didn't think you'd believe me."

Michelle let out a scream so loud and sharp, it almost cracked every window in the living room. Amaryllis ran to the telephone and called Nicholas. "Daddy, it's Michelle. You gotta come over here."

Nicholas could hear Michelle screaming and crying through the telephone. "What's wrong with her?"

"Something has happened with James," Amaryllis responded.

"I'm on my way." Nicholas disconnected the call and rushed to Michelle's house.

Amaryllis held Michelle tight in her arms and rocked her back and forth while they waited for their father.

Twenty minutes later, Nicholas stormed into the living

room using his emergency key. He rushed and knelt next to Michelle. "What happened, Baby Girl? Is James all right?"

Nicholas referring to Michelle as his baby girl infuriated Amaryllis. She moved away and allowed her father to console his precious daughter.

Amaryllis sat and listened as Michelle read the letters that came with puzzle pieces to Nicholas. "All this time, Daddy, I thought it was Jodie playing a joke on me."

Nicholas studied the picture and completed puzzle Michelle had put together. "Baby Girl, there's got to be an explanation. James wouldn't do this."

The more Nicholas referred to Michelle as Baby Girl, the more ticked off Amaryllis became. And the fact that he defended James angered her even more. "What kind of explanation? We got proof that James is a dog," Amaryllis shouted.

Nicholas looked at her. "You don't know James like I do. He's an honest man and wouldn't do anything like this."

"Oh, yeah? Well, what about him coming on to *me*?"

Nicholas refused to believe her. "What? No way."

"It's true. James came on to me *many* times, but I didn't tell Michelle because I knew it would hurt her."

Nicholas stood firm. "I can't believe that; not James."

"You don't believe me?" Amaryllis shrieked.

"Amaryllis, Michelle needs to talk to James."

"Talk to him about what? You're looking at the proof. He can't talk his way out of this."

Nicholas thought Amaryllis was taking Michelle's problem a bit too personally. "You act like you're the one marrying James. Why are *you* so upset?"

"Because Michelle is my sister and when she hurts, I hurt."

Nicholas looked at Michelle. "What do you wanna do?"

Michelle blew her nose in the Kleenex Amaryllis had given her. "Get James over here, Daddy."

Nicholas was glad that Michelle requested to see James. He himself wanted to get to the bottom of the situation. He called James on his cellular telephone and asked him to come to Michelle's house right away. James informed Nicholas that he was finishing up an investigation at a crime scene and that he'd be there within the hour.

Nicholas sat with Michelle on the sofa and pulled her into his arms. "James is on his way. I'm sure he can clear everything up."

Amaryllis sat in a Lay-Z-Boy recliner, opposite of them. The three of them were in silence for forty-five minutes, with the exception of Michelle's sniffles and occasional nose blowing, until James walked in Michelle's front door all smiles carrying a dozen roses. He saw Nicholas sitting on the sofa with his arms around Michelle.

James looked at her and knew she'd been crying. "Mickey, what's wrong?"

Michelle stood, walked over to him and slapped his face. James lost his balance and dropped the roses, stunned by Michelle's blow. "What was that for?"

Michelle pointed to the picture and puzzle on the cock-tail table. "For that."

James caressed his stinging jaw and went to the cock-tail table to see what Michelle was pointing at. He picked up the picture and looked at it. He saw the woman, he saw his sofa and he saw his own face, but he didn't under-stand how it could be. "What is this?"

Amaryllis spoke up. "You tell *us*, James. What is it?"

James was dumbfounded. "This ain't me, Mickey. I didn't do this."

Michelle looked at him. "James, can you honestly look at me and say that it's not you?"

"Yes. I don't know what this is. Where did you get this?"

"Never mind that. You claim it's not you, so I guess the picture is lying, right?"

"Mickey, I promise before God that this is not me. I mean, it's me, but I didn't do this Mickey. I didn't."

Amaryllis wasn't about to let him talk his way out of this. "Tell her what you did to me, James."

Nicholas still didn't believe Amaryllis' accusations. "Amaryllis, shut up."

"No, Daddy, Michelle needs to hear this. James, tell her about the times you tried to kiss me."

James started to sweat. "What the heck are you talking about?"

"Tell Michelle about the time you came over here when you knew she was working late and brought oysters and candles with you."

James couldn't believe this was happening to him. "Amaryllis, you're the one who came on to *me* that night."

"You can't turn this on me, James, I already told Michelle everything."

James was furious. "What are you talking about? You're lying, Amaryllis."

Michelle looked at James. "If Amaryllis came on to you, why didn't you tell me about it?"

It was at this exact moment that James wished he'd taken his pastor's advice. He should've done exactly what his Bishop told him to do. He advised James to tell Michelle about Amaryllis' actions and he chose not to do so. James had been forewarned that this scene would play out exactly as it was being played. "Because I was afraid you wouldn't believe me, Mickey."

New tears started to stream down Michelle's face. "I thought you loved me. All this time, you've been playing me for a fool. Is this what I've been waiting for all of my life? Is this the thanks I get for saving myself for you? What happened, James? You got tired of waiting? You couldn't wait for our wedding night? Is sex *that* important to you?"

Michelle's words hit James like a ton of bricks. She was breaking his heart. James stepped to her and tried to hug her. "Mickey, I can't explain this. It never happened."

Michelle got very upset and yelled. "Stop the lies, James! You're busted. It's you in the picture. Is it not your face?"

He didn't answer her.

Michelle snatched the picture from James' hand and held it close to his eyes. She practically screamed at him. "Is this your face?"

"Yes, I mean no, I mean yes, it's me in the picture, but I didn't do this and I don't know who that woman is."

Michelle forcefully pushed James' chest. "Get out of my house."

Again, he tried to hug her and she started punching him. "Get out, get out!"

Nicholas jumped in between them. "James, maybe you better go."

"But, Nick, I—" James started.

"Leave. Now," Nicholas demanded.

James looked at Michelle through teary eyes. His voice was broken. "I would never, ever do anything to hurt you. You know that. You have to believe that, Mickey. You have to believe in me."

Michelle didn't want to hear anymore of James' lies. She screamed one last time, "Get out!"

James hung his head and walked out the door, accidentally treading over the roses he'd bought for Michelle. Nicholas guided Michelle to the sofa and sat her down.

Amaryllis went into the kitchen for more Kleenex and a glass of water for Michelle then returned to the living room. "Shh; it's okay, sis. It's better you found out now than *after* the wedding." Amaryllis handed Michelle the glass of water.

Nicholas looked at her. "Leave me alone with her, Amaryllis."

Amaryllis wasn't done trashing James. She had plenty more to say. "She needs me right now."

"I'm here with her now, leave us alone," Nicholas demanded.

Amaryllis went upstairs, but when she was out of view, she listened to what they were saying.

"Baby Girl, something doesn't add up. You know James would never do anything like this," Nicholas reasoned.

Michelle blew her puffy red nose into the Kleenex. "How can you explain the picture, Daddy?"

"I don't know. Maybe someone put James' face on another man's body or something. With the way technology is nowadays, anything can be altered."

"But who would take the time and do such a thing? Anyway, it's his sofa, Daddy."

"I understand, but you should hear James' side of the story."

"No, I don't wanna talk to him." Michelle ran upstairs crying.

Amaryllis ducked in the second floor bathroom. She heard Michelle's bedroom door slam. Nicholas grabbed his keys and left the town home. When Amaryllis heard both doors shut, she patted herself on the back for a job well done.

Her initial intention was to snatch James from Michelle. But when James refused her advances, Amaryllis became bitter and vindictive. She no longer wanted him for herself, but instead, set out to destroy his relationship with Michelle. Since James didn't want Amaryllis, she had fixed it so that Michelle no longer wanted him.

James called Michelle at least twenty times that night but she refused to talk to him. On the very last call James made to the house, Amaryllis answered and informed him that Michelle was done with him and the wedding was off.

Chapter 14

At lunchtime on Thursday, Amaryllis poked her head into Michelle's office. "I'm going to the deli for a sandwich. You want anything?"

Michelle didn't look up from the paperwork she was reading. "No, thanks."

Five minutes after Amaryllis left, the telephone rang. Michelle looked at the caller identification and saw that it was a Chicago call from Price & Associates.

"So, you still got a job, huh?" a female's voice asked.

Michelle frowned. "I beg your pardon?"

"You heard me. Your sister ain't kicked you to the curb yet?"

Michelle had no clue who this woman was or what she was talking about. "I think you have the wrong number."

Bridgette knew Amaryllis' voice. "Don't try and act like you don't know who I am, Amaryllis. It's me, Bridgette, your home girl."

Now that she heard the name, Michelle remembered Amaryllis mentioning someone named Bridgette, a co-worker, from Chicago. "Oh, Bridgette, this isn't Amaryllis."

"Girl, stop playing, you think I don't know your voice? Who are you trying to fool?"

"I'm Michelle, Amaryllis' *sister.*"

Bridgette chuckled. "Oh, okay, you're Michelle today, huh? What happened, Amaryllis? You wanted to live your sister's life so badly that you hit her over the head, buried the body some place, dyed your skin, adopted her voice and took over her business?"

Michelle was totally at a loss to what Bridgette was saying. "I beg your pardon?"

"You beg my pardon? Is that what they teach you to say in Vegas? All I wanna know is if Michelle figured out what you've done yet."

It was clear that Bridgette didn't understand that she was on the phone with the wrong sister, but Michelle was dying to know what she was talking about. "What's to figure out?"

"That you purposely put your name on her wedding invitations, and how you set her man up to take those pictures by drugging him. I bet she doesn't even know that you're the one who sent the puzzle, does she?"

Michelle's eyes grew wide, her heart started to race and her palms got sweaty. She dropped the telephone then stood and leaned forward on her desk. All of a sudden, she couldn't breathe. Her lungs were completely empty and she was gasping for air that wasn't there. She looked around the room and saw it spinning all around her.

Michelle got dizzy, staggered backward and fell into her chair. Her back was drenched with sweat and her blouse was clinging to her. She felt like she had the flu. She was chilled to the bone, yet burning up with fever-like temperatures. She hadn't realized she was crying until a tear dripped from her chin. "Oh my God, no. No, Jesus, no, no, no. Not my sister. Not, Amaryllis."

Michelle was distraught and disgusted. She grabbed her purse and keys and walked to the elevator. It wasn't coming fast enough, so she took the stairs two at a time, something she'd never done. When Michelle got to the driver's side of her Jaguar, she vomited. She wiped her mouth with her sleeve then got in her car and sped out of the parking lot.

Michelle got on the freeway, but her tears made it difficult for her to see where she was going. She got to Nicholas's house in less than twenty minutes and recklessly drove one wheel up on the curb. Michelle stumbled out of the driver's seat and left her door open. While running to the front door, her legs gave out and she fell to the ground, but managed to crawl the rest of the way to her father's front door. Michelle pulled herself up and banged on the door like a maniac. When he didn't answer right away, she started screaming and crying. "Daddy, please open the door. Daddy . . . Daddy!"

Still there was no answer. Michelle fell to her knees, holding her stomach. "Please, Daddy; please open the door."

Just then, Nicholas yanked his door open, dressed in his terry cloth robe. He saw his daughter kneeling and crying. "Baby Girl?"

Michelle looked up at him. "Daddy, what took you so long?"

"I was in the shower. What's wrong?"

Michelle couldn't say anything. She looked at Nicholas and shook her head from side to side. "I can't breathe, Daddy. I can't breathe."

Nicholas bent down to helped Michelle stand, then pulled her into the house. Michelle was shaking uncontrollably. She still couldn't get enough air into her lungs.

Nicholas saw that she was short of breath. He pulled her into his arms and held her very close to him. If Michelle didn't get control of her breathing, Nicholas feared she would pass out. "Shhh, calm down and breathe."

"But, Daddy—"

"Calm down first. Please don't faint on me."

Nicholas walked Michelle into the kitchen and sat her down at the table. He filled a glass with water from the sink and gave it to her. He saw that her hands were shaking, so he held the glass to her lips. "Take a sip."

Michelle did as she was told and leaned back in the chair. Nicholas set the glass on the counter and sat across from her. "Now tell me what happened."

She told her father about the telephone call she'd received from Amaryllis' friend, Bridgette. When she was done, she was breathless. Nicholas came and knelt in front of her and pulled her into his arms.

"I don't wanna hear the I-told-you-so's, Daddy," Michelle told him before he could even get started.

"Baby Girl, you should know me better than that. Have you spoken to James?"

"No, I left the firm and drove straight here. Daddy, I took Amaryllis' side over his and I accused him of lying and cheating. But James was right all along. I doubt if he'll ever talk to me again."

"James is a good man, Michelle." Nichols stood and walked out of the kitchen.

"Where are you going?"

"To get dressed."

Five minutes later, Nicholas was standing at the kitchen door dressed in a nylon jogging suit and K Swiss gym shoes on his feet. With his keys in his hand, he said to Michelle, "Come on."

"Where are we going?"

"You'll see."

When they got in Nicholas' car, he turned to his daughter and asked, "What's James' number at the precinct?"

"Why, Daddy? What are you gonna say to him?"

"Just give me the number."

Michelle reluctantly recited the number and watched her father dial.

"Homicide, Detective Bradley here." Michelle could hear her fiancé's voice from where she sat. The sadness in his voice broke her heart.

"James, this is Nick. Don't ask any questions, just drop whatever you're doing and go to Michelle's house. She's with me and we'll meet you there.

Nicholas and Michelle got to the town home first. Once inside, he went straight to the third floor and Michelle was close on his heels. He turned the knob on Amaryllis' bedroom door and found that it was locked. "Where's the key?" he asked Michelle.

"There isn't a key. I never lock any of the bedroom doors."

"Stand back." Nicholas took two steps backward and kicked the door with his right foot. It flew open and banged against the wall. They walked in and Nicholas went to Amaryllis' dresser drawer.

"What are you looking for, Daddy?"

"I won't know 'til I find it."

While he was rummaging through the drawers, Michelle went over to Amaryllis' closet and opened shoe boxes and looked in pockets, not even certain what she was searching for.

Nicholas was throwing everything onto the floor, searching through her clothes. He found a bottle of pills with *Vicodin* written on the bottom of it. He held it up for Michelle to see. "What's this?"

Michelle looked at the bottle. "That's Amaryllis' medication."

"For what?"

"For when she was in pain."

"Vicodin doesn't take pain away, it knocks you out," Nicholas said. He looked at the date for when it was filled. "This prescription is almost two months old and it's for fifteen pills."

Michelle walked to Nicholas, took the bottle from his hand and looked at it. "She hasn't taken these in the last two months. She's been bright eyed and bushy tailed." Michelle noticed that the pharmacy listed on the bottle was located in Las Vegas. She remembered Amaryllis' original bottle of Vicodin had been filled by a doctor in Chicago. Michelle also remembered dumping the pills down the sink and filling the bottle with regular strength Tylenol. She opened the bottle to examine the pills and was shocked to see five authentic Vicodin pills.

"Did you find anything in the closet?"

"No," Michelle replied, still stunned about the new pills.

James walked in the front door and yelled, "Nick, you in here?"

"Come up to the third floor, James," Nicholas yelled back.

James obeyed and walked into Amaryllis' room and saw that it was turned upside down. "What's going on? Are you all right, Mickey?" James wore a horrid expression on his face.

Michelle ran into his arms. "James, baby, I'm so sorry."

James didn't know what happened or why she was apologizing. He watched as Nicholas got down on his knees and looked under the bed, but saw nothing. Nicholas then stood and walked away. He stopped abruptly and turned back around and stared at the mattress.

"James, help me flip this mattress," Nicholas said, already moving toward the bed.

Amaryllis was exposed. Underneath her mattress was a blond wig, a small camera, a set of keys and an envelope.

James grabbed the wig and held it up in front of Michelle. "Doesn't this look familiar, Mickey?"

"That's the hair from the lady in the picture," Michelle said.

James picked up the keys and examined them. "These are my house keys."

Nicholas opened the envelope and saw something he didn't wanna see. "Oh, my God." He gave the picture to Michelle.

She looked at it and started crying again. "Another picture?"

James pulled Michelle in his arms and comforted her. "You see, Mickey, I've been telling you the truth. But I still don't understand how she got me to take the pictures."

Michelle looked at the pill bottle in her hand then looked at Nicholas and James. "Now we do." Michelle filled James in on what Bridgette unknowingly disclosed to her about Amaryllis drugging him.

James became enraged. "So, you realize that Amaryllis lied about me coming on to her. It never happened, Mickey."

Michelle looked deeply into James' eyes. "Yes, I do realize that now. And I'm so sorry for not believing you in the first place. Please forgive me."

James kissed Michelle's forehead softly then chuckled. "I gotta admit, Amaryllis had strong incriminating evidence against me. I've never known pictures to lie but I'm glad to know that that's not the case in this matter."

Nicholas took the bottle from Michelle and showed James the date on it. "What did you do on this day?"

"That was two months ago. I don't remember."

"Honey, where's your log that you write everything in?" Michelle asked.

James reached in his shirt pocket and pulled out his logbook. He turned to the date on the pill bottle. "That was the day Alexander and I flew to Detroit to pick up two prisoners; remember, Mickey?"

"Yeah, that's also the day I was at your house with the carpet cleaners," Michelle recalled.

Nicholas spoke to Michelle. "Did Amaryllis work that day?"

"Yeah."

"Do you remember what she did that night?"

"Nothing unusual." Michelle thought for a moment. "Oh, yeah; that's the night she went to a book club meeting with some ladies from the firm."

"Baby Girl, why don't you call one of the ladies and verify if Amaryllis was there."

Michelle picked up the telephone on the nightstand and called the firm. The receptionist answered. "Hi, Angela, it's Michelle. Put me through to Jessica in the file room please."

"Sure, Michelle," Angela obliged.

Michelle heard elevator music for five seconds.

"Jessica speaking."

"Jessica, it's Michelle."

"Hi."

"Did you host a book club meeting at your house about two months ago?"

"Yes, I did."

"Was my sister, Amaryllis, there?"

"Amaryllis was invited, but said she had something else more interesting to do that evening."

"That's why she couldn't remember the title of the book

when I asked her about it. Thanks, Jessica." Michelle disconnected the call.

The three of them stood in Amaryllis' bedroom and concluded that Amaryllis had planned to destroy the relationship between Michelle and James because she wanted him for herself.

James looked at the picture again. "That's why I missed roll call, Mickey. She drugged me. Remember how out of it I was when I got to your office the next day?"

"Yeah, I remember." Michelle looked at the picture and noticed something. "What's that?"

James studied the photo she was holding. "What?"

Michelle pointed to Amaryllis' butt. "That dark spot on her behind."

Nicholas took the picture from her and looked at it. "It looks like a tattoo of a rose or something." No sooner than he said the words, something dawned on Nicholas. "Oh, no. It can't be."

"What is it, Daddy?"

"I could be wrong, and I hope to God I am, but the lady that stripped at James' bachelor party had the exact same tattoo *and* wig."

Michelle got angrier by the moment. "This heifer had the gall to show up at my man's party and get naked in front of him? And you too, Daddy; her own father? That nasty cow. I want her out of my house, right now."

The wheels in Nicholas' head were turning. "I know, Baby Girl, but humor me first."

"What do you mean?"

"If you can hold on a little longer, we can beat Amaryllis at her own game. Even though we have all the evidence we need to know that she's under the wig in these pictures, let's make one more confirmation."

"I want her out of my house, Daddy," Michelle insisted.

"Baby Girl, do this for me. Just be cool until she gets home from work. Wait until she gets in the shower, then walk in on her and check to see if she's got the tattoo."

"And then what?" Michelle asked.

"Then you handle your business," James stated matter-of-factly.

At six-thirty P.M., Amaryllis drove Michelle's Navigator into the driveway and opened the overhead door to the garage. In the spaces where she and Michelle park were Nicholas and James' cars. *What are they doing here and where's Michelle's car?*

She parked in the driveway, and when she opened the front door, she smelled food and heard laughing coming from the kitchen. Her first thought was to head straight upstairs, but curiosity was killing the cat. Her father and James were there. What did it mean?

Amaryllis walked to the kitchen doorway and saw Nicholas, James and Michelle eating mustard and turnip greens, hot water cornbread, homemade macaroni and cheese, honey baked ham, sweet potatoes and corn on the cob. In the center of the table sat a pitcher of grape Kool-Aid. When Amaryllis saw the Kool-Aid, she glanced at James who was literally licking his fingers. She remembered Michelle telling her that she'd never cook like this for James until they were married. And if the wedding was off, why was he there?

Michelle looked at her sister and it took all that was within her to keep her spiritual composure. "Hey, sis. You hungry?"

"That's quite a spread. What's going on?" Amaryllis asked, confusion written all over her face.

James answered. "My *fiancé* and I were just telling Nick about our honeymoon plans in Hawaii."

"So, the wedding is back on?" Amaryllis asked, wondering how her plan could have backfired.

"Yep," James answered. "I've apologized to Mickey for cheating on her and she's forgiven me. Ain't God good?" he chuckled.

Amaryllis was furious. "Michelle, once a cheat, always a cheat."

Now it was Nicholas' turn to get in on the conversation. "You would know, wouldn't you?"

Amaryllis looked at her father then turned and walked away. When she was out of hearing range, Michelle looked at Nicholas. "Daddy, why did you say that? You almost gave us away."

"I couldn't help it," he replied as he inserted a forkful of macaroni and cheese into his mouth.

Amaryllis unlocked and opened the door to her bedroom and found it just the way she'd left it that morning. Before she got home, Nicholas and James were able to repair the lock on her door. The first thing she did was check under her mattress. Everything was in its place. She went into her bathroom, closed the door behind her and started the water in the shower. Five minutes later, Michelle yanked the shower curtain back and saw exactly what she was looking for.

Amaryllis didn't know what to think. "Michelle, what is wrong with you?"

Michelle stopped the water. "You are a manipulative, ruthless and vindictive human being and I want you out of my house, *now*."

"What are you talking about?" Amaryllis asked, reaching for a towel.

"I'm talking about you moving into my house and working for me, pretending to love me and all the while, trying to destroy me. You've got five minutes to get out of my house and the clock is ticking."

Michelle left the bathroom and slammed the door. Amaryllis stood in the shower wondering how Michelle had found out. What was she going to do now? There was nothing else for her to do but pack her things and head back to Chicago, so that's exactly what she would do.

An hour later, Amaryllis strolled down the stairs with one suitcase in her hand. Nicholas, Michelle and James were standing in the living room, waiting for her to make her exit. Amaryllis didn't say anything, but then again, what could she say? She walked to the front door and opened it. Michelle called her name, and when Amaryllis turned around, Michelle was in her face.

"There are two things that I don't tolerate people messing with. And that's my chocolate and my man." Michelle balled up her fist and hit Amaryllis across her nose so hard that it sent her sister stumbling backward and she fell onto the porch. But Amaryllis wasn't going down without a fight. She collected herself and was getting ready to come back at Michelle.

Michelle stood flatfooted in the doorway, ready to go one-on-one with her sister. "Come on with it. I'd hit you in your chest so hard, your *momma* would cough." When Michelle put emphasis on the word 'momma,' her neck danced.

Amaryllis didn't move.

Michelle picked up Amaryllis' suitcase and threw it out on the porch. "The fact that I'm saved worked in your favor; 'cause if I wasn't, I'd whip your—"

"Baby Girl!" Nicholas interjected. He was stunned at what his daughter had almost said.

Michelle slammed the door closed. She turned around

and saw James and her father standing with an I-don't-believe-you-did-that expression on their faces. She looked at them both. "God allowed me that."

Nicholas looked out of the living room and saw Amaryllis walking down the street with her suitcase in her hand. With her other hand, she held her swelling nose.

Chapter 15

Amaryllis checked into the Swan Lake Hotel. On the twentieth floor, she opened the curtains and looked down at the people walking along the strip. For the life of her, Amaryllis couldn't figure out how Michelle had found out. Everything was working out exactly the way she planned. She sat down on the bed and called Bridgette. "Girl, guess what happened."

"Amaryllis, I am so sorry," Bridgette said nervously.

"What are you talking about?"

"I thought it was you playing games. You sound just like her."

"Like who?" Amaryllis asked. She wondered what Bridgette was talking about.

"Michelle."

"Michelle?"

"Yeah, when she answered the telephone today, I thought she was you."

Amaryllis massaged her left temple. "Bridgette, you're going in circles. You talked to Michelle today?"

"I called the firm this afternoon and she answered. You two sound exactly the same. I thought I was talking to you. I asked if your sister figured out what you'd done yet and Michelle pretended to be you. She asked what was to figure out and I told her."

Amaryllis panicked and raised her voice. "You told her what?"

"Everything you told me."

"Everything?"

"Everything from changing the wedding invitations to drugging her fiancé to sending her the puzzle. I heard Michelle scream, then I knew that it wasn't you on the telephone."

Amaryllis closed her eyes. "Bridgette, do you have any idea what you've done?"

"What *I've* done?" Bridgette became defensive. "Yeah, Michelle kicked me out of her house tonight."

"You know what, Amaryllis? You've brought this on yourself. Did you really think that you were gonna get away with what you were doing?"

"I *had* gotten away with it, Bridgette, until you messed it up. Michelle punched me in my nose."

"Oh no, you're not gonna blame this on me. This mess is your own fault. I told you in the beginning to leave your sister's man alone. Why can't you find your own man, Amaryllis? I mean you're a beautiful woman."

"I was working on making James mine."

"From what you told me, the man couldn't stand you. He purposely wouldn't look at you or talk to you. That's a sure sign that he didn't want to be bothered. Think about it. You had to drug the man just to get him in a compromising position. Why can't you get the message that he doesn't want you?"

"Bridgette, as fine as I am, every man wants me. You said it yourself; I'm beautiful."

"Humph, then along came James."

Bridgette's response ticked Amaryllis off and she slammed down the telephone. She walked to the window and again looked down at the people walking. Her eyes were drawn across the street to the neon flashing lights in front of a casino. It had been a long time since she had sat at a Blackjack table. There was no sense in worrying about James and Michelle tonight. What was done was done. She thought that a nice round of Blackjack would clear her mind. Amaryllis dismissed all thoughts of her problems and grabbed her purse and room key, then exited her room.

It was a lucky night for Amaryllis. She sat down at the Blackjack table with three hundred dollars and wound up with three thousand. Satisfied that she hadn't lost her skills, she decided to call it quits. Back on the twentieth floor of the Swan Lake Hotel, Amaryllis inserted her key card into its slot and opened the door.

A half hour later, a waitress was delivering room service to a room across the hall from Amaryllis' room. As she was pushing the cart toward the designated room, she looked across to Amaryllis' and saw a foot in the doorway, keeping the door ajar. She slowly walked to the door and pushed it opened. That's when her piercing screams had hotel room doors opening left and right to see what was going on. There on the floor, lay Amaryllis, with a pool of blood surrounding her.

Michelle, James and Nicholas were enjoying some of Michelle's peach cobbler with homemade vanilla ice cream when James' cellular phone rang. "James, it's Alex. Where are you?"

James could tell that Alexander was anxious. "I'm at Mickey's. Why?"

"You need to come to the Swan Lake Hotel right now."

"I'm off duty, Alex, and so are you, man. What are you doing at the Swan Lake Hotel?"

"Can Michelle hear you talking?" Alexander asked.

"Yeah."

James listened as Alexander explained why he needed to make his way to the Hotel. "I'm on my way." James ended the call and tried his best to keep a straight face.

"What is it, honey?" Michelle asked.

"That was Alex. He needs my help at a crime scene. I won't be long." He stood and kissed Michelle then looked at Nicholas and motioned for him to meet him in the living room. Michelle gathered plates and walked to the sink. In the living room, James relayed to Nicholas the details of Alexander's call.

A few minutes later, Michelle called out. "Daddy, you want coffee?" She didn't get an answer. Going into the living room, she found both James and Nicholas gone. The two had left together and she was home alone.

An officer tried to prevent Nicholas from following James into the hotel. James flashed his badge. "He's with me."

"But, Detective, no one is allowed—"

"I said, he's with me."

The officer stepped aside. James and Nicholas entered the hotel and took the elevator to the twentieth floor. When the elevator doors opened, they were greeted with yellow crime scene tape and police officers working.

Alexander approached them. "James, I'm glad you're

here, man." He turned his attention to Nicholas. "Nick, I'm
sorry."

Nicholas looked at Alexander. "What happened to her?"

"It looks like robbery and attempted murder."

"So, she's not . . ." Nicholas' words trailed off. He could-
n't ask the question.

"She's alive, but it doesn't look good. She was beaten
badly and she's lost a lot of blood. The paramedics are
working on her. Had the waitress not found her when she
did, Amaryllis would have bled to death." Alexander
looked around and noticed Michelle wasn't with them.
"Where's Michelle?"

"At home. She doesn't know," James said.

Alexander escorted them into Amaryllis' hotel room.
There were three paramedics tending to her. One placed
an oxygen mask on her face and another was inserting an
I.V. into her arm.

James walked over to the third paramedic. "I'm Detective Bradley. How is she?"

"She just slipped into a coma. I doubt if she makes it.
She's lost a lot of blood."

They carried Amaryllis out on a stretcher past Nicholas.
James approached him. "Nick, I'm sorry. She's in a coma
and the paramedics aren't optimistic."

Even though Amaryllis wreaked havoc wherever she
went, and even though she was wrong for what she had
done to her own sister, Nicholas still loved his daughter
and couldn't help but whisper a prayer to God for her re-
covery and healing.

Michelle opened the door to see a distraught Nicholas.

"Daddy, where did you go and where is James? I've
been calling both of your cell phones and left messages."

Nicholas walked in and sat on the sofa. "Come sit with me, Baby Girl."

Michelle's heart started to race. Every time Nicholas told her to come and sit with him, it usually meant bad news. She slowly walked and sat down. "Did something happen to James?"

Nicholas took her hands into his. "No, it's not James."

"What is it then?"

He silently prayed for the right words to tell her. "It's Amaryllis."

"I don't want to hear anything about her." Michelle stood to walk away, but Nicholas grabbed her arm.

"She was attacked and robbed at the Swan Lake Hotel."

Michelle's eyes grew wide. "Attacked how?"

"She was brutally beaten in her hotel room and her purse was stolen. By the time she was found, she had been lying in a pool of blood for quite some time. She's lost a tremendous amount of blood and the paramedics don't think she'll make it through the night."

"No, Daddy, no."

"James is at Vegas Memorial with her now."

"Take me to her." Michelle grabbed her keys and purse, and followed her father's lead.

Michelle rushed into the intensive care unit with Nicholas close behind. James and Alexander were standing outside Amaryllis' hospital room when they saw Michelle running toward them. She ran to James and buried her face in his arms. "How's my sister?"

"Mickey, the doctor just left her." James paused before continuing. "She's not going to make it."

Michelle's knees collapsed. James barely caught her from hitting the floor.

"I gotta see her, James. I wanna see my sister. I don't care what the doctor said. Jesus can still say 'yes.' "

Nicholas escorted Michelle into the room. Amaryllis lay in bed unconscious, with many machines attached to her. Michelle saw tubes taped to her arms. She pulled up a chair and sat next to the bed and grabbed Amaryllis' hand. "Why, sis? Why does it have to be this way?"

Nicholas stood behind Michelle and put his hand on her shoulder. Michelle patted his hand. "Leave me alone with her, Daddy."

Nicholas squeezed Michelle's shoulder and left the room. Michelle closed her eyes. "My God, I know you're a miracle worker and I need you to perform one right now . . ."

Nicholas, James and Alexander stood outside of Amaryllis' room for an hour with Michelle inside. James poked his head into the room. "Mickey, I hate to leave you at a time like this, but Alex and I have to go to another crime scene."

Michelle didn't move or respond. James walked over to her and saw her eyes closed and her lips moving silently while she held Amaryllis' hand. He left the room and told Nicholas to call him if anything changed. Nicholas peeped in at Michelle, sitting by her sister's side.

Amaryllis began to dream.

The year was nineteen eighty-four. Amaryllis saw herself at eight years old, being taken out of school in handcuffs for pushing a nun down a flight of stairs.

Imps began attacking Amaryllis. Michelle could see her lifeless body being pulled in every direction.

The year was nineteen eighty-six. Amaryllis heard little Karla Monroe in the shower at day camp, scream-

ing and crying because her hair was falling out due to the fact that Amaryllis had put hair remover in her shampoo.

Amaryllis' flesh was being torn from her bones as she lay in a coma. Michelle saw tears streaming from her eyes down to her ears.

The year was nineteen ninety. Amaryllis saw her neighbor, Mr. Taylor, being carried away by ambulance because two goons jumped him in the alley after his wife anonymously found out he was cheating.

Michelle watched as her sister's body convulsed. The imps had inhaled her skin from her lifeless body.

Amaryllis saw herself fully grown, walking down the street in the rain when a thunderclap spoke to her. "YOU ARE A BAD SEED." Suddenly, a lightning bolt stretched out from the sky and struck her and knocked her to the ground.

An alarm sounded on one of the machines. Michelle looked at it and saw Amaryllis had flat lined. Michelle began screaming and hollering. "Oh God, no. Please, God. Please, don't take my sister from me. Please, Jesus, please."

Two nurses rushed into the room and shooed Michelle out into the hallway. She stood and watched through the window of the door as the doctor and attending nurses work on reviving Amaryllis. Nicholas stood behind Michelle and watched as well.

"Are you praying, Daddy?," Michelle asked her father.

"Yes, I am," he replied sadly.

The medical team were able to silence the machine's alarm after two minutes. After adjusting the tubes in Amaryllis' arms and chest, they allowed Michelle back into the room. No sooner than when Michelle sat next to her again, Amaryllis' eyes opened. She looked at Michelle sitting beside her praying and she squeezed her hand. Michelle saw Amaryllis had awaken and began praising God. Two nurses came back into the room and asked Michelle to step out while they tended to Amaryllis.

At the nurses' station, Michelle left strict instructions. "Please remove my name as next of kin for Amaryllis Price. Our father, Nicholas Price, is to be contacted for anything regarding Amaryllis."

Having prayed and pleaded with God to bring her sister back, Michelle felt her job as a loyal sister was complete. She'd done her part. Amaryllis was alive. Michelle asked Nicholas to drive her home and he did.

Once she was cared for, Amaryllis asked the nurse to send her sister in. The nurse reported to Amaryllis that Michelle and Nicholas had departed. She asked Amaryllis if she wanted her father to be reached to return to the hospital.

"No," was Amaryllis's answer. For the first time in her life, she truly felt all alone.

Chapter 16

Early Sunday morning, three days after Amaryllis was admitted into the hospital and six days until Michelle and James' wedding, Nicholas arrived at the hospital. Amaryllis' doctor had just signed her release papers and was leaving the room as Nicholas was walking in. She was sitting on the bed, dressed and facing the window. Nicholas stood quietly for a moment and watched his daughter, wondering how anyone with a pumping heart could be so evil and do what she'd done.

"Amaryllis?"

His voice startled her and she turned to look at her father. "Hi, Daddy. I didn't hear you come in. Where's Michelle?"

"Why are you asking for her?"

"I thought she'd be the one to come and take me home."

"After what you've done to her? Do you have any idea how you almost destroyed your sister?"

"Daddy, this kind of thing happens everyday. Michelle is a big girl. She'll get over it."

At her words, Nicholas was stunned. He knew Amaryllis was coldhearted, but to hear those words flow nonchalantly from her lips truly amazed him. "Amaryllis, when your mother and I divorced, Michelle and I moved to Las Vegas. I know I wasn't a big part of your teenage and young adult years, so I need you to tell me what happened to make you behave this way."

"You just answered your own question."

"*I'm* to blame for you making folks' lives miserable?"

Amaryllis didn't answer her father. Instead, she asked a question of her own. "Why didn't you bring me here to live with you and Michelle?"

"Amaryllis, I tried to get custody of you, but Veronica fought me tooth and nail."

"You knew Veronica was screwed up in the head. I knew all about her running the streets and selling dope behind the house in the alley. Do you know that if I didn't want to go to school, she didn't make me?"

For the first time ever, Nicholas saw emotion in Amaryllis. Tears flowed from her lower eyelids.

"I'm sorry, Amaryllis. I will accept the blame. I could have visited more, but you are a grown woman now. I don't care what kind of upbringing you had, what you did to Michelle was wrong."

"I am who I am, Daddy."

He stood and looked at her. From his suit's interior jacket pocket, he withdrew a white envelope and gave it to her."

"What's this?"

"It's a one-way ticket to Chicago. Your plane leaves in four hours. There's a taxicab downstairs with all of your belongings waiting to take you to the airport."

Nicholas turned to leave then stopped and turned around. "I wasn't gonna say anything because Michelle asked me not to, but you need to know that you were as good as dead when the ambulance brought you here. It's only by the grace of God that the waitress found you in time. When your sister was told that she was the only one who matched your blood type, she wasted no time offering her veins for your sake. And she didn't stop there, Amaryllis.

"While you were in a coma, Michelle was here kneeling by your bed, praying for you. In spite of everything you've done to her, she still loves you. She took you into her home when you were broken and beaten. She bathed you, literally fed you with a spoon, nurtured you back to health and you show your gratitude by doing the worst thing a woman could ever do to her own sister. Every time I turn around, I hear about you doin' tha fool. And every time I warned Michelle about getting too comfortable with you, she defended you. She trusted you, Amaryllis. Is your life *that* miserable that you can't help but make everybody else's life miserable too?"

Amaryllis looked at her father as though she wasn't phased by anything he was saying to her.

"Do you feel any remorse? Have you *any* shame for the things you've done?" Nicholas didn't wait for an answer, he knew what it would be anyway. "I'm late for church. Make sure you're on that plane."

Amaryllis watched her father leave and looked down at the airplane ticket. Something wet dripped on it. She looked at the ceiling for a leak but her vision was blurred. It dawned on her that it was her own tears dripping onto the ticket.

The nurse came into the room with a wheelchair and saw her. "Why the tears? You're supposed to be happy to leave this place."

When Amaryllis got down to the cab, she gave the driver the address to Praise Temple Church of God.

"I'm sorry, ma'am. I have specific instructions to take you directly to the airport," the driver reported.

"How much did he pay you?"

"Fifty bucks."

"I'll double it."

Amaryllis entered the sanctuary and saw Bishop Graham preaching in the pulpit. She saw Michelle sitting on the right side of the church on the second pew from the front. Next to her sat Nicholas with his arm around her shoulders. James was sitting in the pulpit and saw Amaryllis the moment she came into the sanctuary. He tried his best to get either Nicholas' or Michelle's attention, but they had their eyes fixed on Bishop Graham.

Amaryllis walked in and sat down on a pew at the rear of the church. She looked at James who had his eyes fixed on her, then she turned her attention to what Bishop Graham was saying. He was at the height of his sermon entitled, "Don't Settle."

"For your entire life, you've been searching for love in all the wrong places. You thought love was in the casinos, but it wasn't. You thought love was in married men's and women's beds, but it wasn't. You thought love was in the nightclubs, but it wasn't," Bishop Graham preached.

Amaryllis glanced around the church to see if anyone was looking at her. Bishop Graham was hitting home and she wondered how much more of her business he was going to tell.

"Have you ever thought about the mess and dirt you've done and God still seems to keep His hand on your life? Some of us know that we should've been dead long ago, but God kept us because He loves us."

The saints were on their feet rejoicing. Bishop Graham was pacing the pulpit as he raised his voice. The organist accompanied him. The louder Bishop Graham preached, the louder the organist played.

"My brothers and sisters, I came to tell you today that you can bind your sin in the name of Jesus. Matthew, chapter sixteen, verse nineteen says, 'I will give you the keys to the kingdom of heaven; and whatever you bind on earth will be bound in heaven, and whatever you loose on earth will be loosed in heaven.'

"The word *bind* means to hinder or to restrict. You've got the power to bind and to loose. The enemy has a way of making you feel like there's no hope for you when you're going through a particular situation. But you can bind that devil that hinders you and loose the blessings of God upon your life."

The congregation was in an uproar. Amaryllis found that she couldn't sit any longer. She joined the saints on their feet and applauded what Bishop Graham was saying.

"Isaiah, chapter fifty-four, verse seventeen says, 'No weapon formed against you will prevail, and you will refute every tongue that accuses you.' That means that anything the devil throws your way shall not prosper. Tell yourselves, I've got the power to bind every devil that attaches itself to me."

A man standing next to Amaryllis started to dance. She moved out of his way and he danced into the aisle. Tears started to stream down her face as she watched the saints rejoice.

Bishop Graham kept on preaching. "Ephesians, chapter three, verse twenty says, 'Now to Him who is able to do immeasurably more than all we ask or imagine, according to His power that is at work within us.' That means that if you trust God, He is able to keep you from falling into the enemy's grip because you have His power in you."

Suddenly, Amaryllis started jumping up and down repeating the words, "I've got the power, I've got the power."

Bishop Graham slowed his heart rate and stood behind the podium and looked out at the congregation. "I don't know who I'm talking to, but I'm talking to somebody in here today. God wants you to know that any stronghold of the enemy cannot attach itself to you if you bind it with His word. Anything the devil puts on you or against you, bind it in the name of Jesus; by the blood of Jesus."

Amaryllis' smeared black mascara made her look like a raccoon, but she didn't care. She knew that it was God who had brought her here today. Her initial reason for coming to the church was to confront Michelle and cause a scene. She wanted to disrupt the service and bring shame to her father. But what was meant for evil was turned for good.

"Young man, you don't have to keep taking drugs. Young lady, you don't have to sell and misuse your body. There is a better life for you. To *loose* means to set free. You have the power and authority to loose yourself from the enemy's plan. Today, I want to encourage God's people and to let you know that the power of God is in you and you don't have to let the devil walk up and down your back. But you can stand flatfooted and let the devil know that he is a liar and the truth is not in him. Know that you are the righteousness of God and you are a joint heir with Jesus Christ."

Amaryllis began to holler out "Amen" and "Thank You Jesus."

"Know ye that the Lord, He is God. Tell yourselves that you won't accept weakness and you won't accept defeat. You can accept the greatness of God that is upon your life. Somebody say, 'Yeah.' "

"Yeah!" the church echoed.

"Shout, 'Yeah.' "

"Yeah!

Bishop Graham hooped. "Saaaaay, 'Yeeeaaahhh.' "

Amaryllis felt the Holy Spirit all over her. Unable to contain herself, she moved out into the center aisle and ran to the front of the church and threw herself at Michelle's feet. Amaryllis wrapped her arms around her sister's legs and it caused Michelle to stumble. She looked down at Amaryllis who was crying and begging for mercy.

"I'm sorry, Michelle, please forgive me. I'm so sorry. I love you, I love you, please forgive me. Please don't turn from me, Michelle, I need you. I need my sister. I ain't got nobody else. Don't nobody love me like you. I'm so sorry, I'm so sorry."

Michelle was crying too. She had already forgiven Amaryllis in her heart, but set her mind to believe that if she never saw her sister again, it wouldn't bother her. But right now, seeing Amaryllis beg for mercy, softened Michelle's hardened heart and she decided not to let the enemy win. At that moment, she was determined to have a relationship with her only sister. She bent down to help Amaryllis stand. She looked into her eyes and saw sincerity and humbleness. Michelle pulled Amaryllis into her arms and squeezed her tight. "I've already forgiven you." Michelle guided Amaryllis to the altar and stood in front of Bishop Graham. "Bishop, my sister is seeking forgiveness from the Lord. Can you please pray for her?"

Before Bishop Graham honored Michelle's request, Amaryllis spoke. "No, that's not what I'm standing here for."

Both Michelle and Bishop Graham looked confused and he asked Amaryllis a question. "If you're not here seeking prayer, then how may I help you, my daughter?"

Amaryllis was crying uncontrollably, but she managed

to pull herself together. "I need you to tell me what I gotta do to get into heaven. What do I need to do to be saved?"

Michelle's eyes rolled to the back of her head and she fell to the floor. James ran out of the pulpit to see about her. Nicholas went to Amaryllis and wrapped his arms around her and cried.

The entire church sent praises up to God.

Two hours later, Amaryllis was sitting in the airport, waiting for her flight number to be called. The church had given her a small Bible as a token of love. She was glancing at scriptures when someone from behind approached her. "Hello, saint."

Amaryllis looked over her shoulder and saw Michelle. She stood and faced her. "Hi. What are you doing here?"

Ordinarily, because of security, Michelle wouldn't have been allowed at the boarding gate without a ticket. She told the security guard that she was an attorney and her client was about to board a plane, but she had crucial information that she needed to share with her client. The guard reluctantly allowed Michelle through.

"I couldn't let the newest member of God's family leave without giving her a proper goodbye, could I?"

Amaryllis stood in front of Michelle. "Thanks, Michelle. That means a lot to me."

Michelle fought back tears. "Listen. In spite of what happened, we are still sisters, you hear me? I told you that we only got each other, so we gotta take care of one another."

Amaryllis's eyes also started to flood. "How can you still love me after what I've done?"

"Amaryllis, no one in this world is perfect. Now that you have a Bible, I want you to read Colossians, chapter three, verse thirteen. It tells us that if we don't forgive others, we won't be forgiven by God."

Just that morning, Amaryllis had crassly told Nicholas that Michelle would get over the hurt she had caused her. Now she had a change of heart. "Yeah, but still, I've done some evil things to you. I can't imagine that I'd be as forgiving if I were in your shoes, Michelle."

"It comes with growth. In time, you'll get there."

Amaryllis's flight number was called. "Well, I guess that's my cue."

Michelle helped her gather her bags. "Make sure you find a church home when you get back to Chicago."

Amaryllis placed her carry on bag on her shoulder and stood still looking at Michelle.

"Why are you looking at me like that?" Michelle asked.

"Because we look almost identical, but we're so different."

"Bishop Graham told you that you have the power to change that."

"Michelle, you are a great example for me to follow in this walk with God and I love you for who you are. If I can be half the woman you are, my life would be just about perfect."

That statement brought more tears to Michelle's eyes and she hugged Amaryllis again. "That's the nicest thing you've ever said to me."

They held each other for a long thirty seconds, then Amaryllis' zone number was called and it was time for her to board. Michelle broke the embrace and held Amaryllis' face in her hands.

"I'm proud of you, little sister."

Tears spilled onto Amaryllis' cheeks as she turned and walked away. When she got to the boarding door that led to the airplane, Michelle called her name and Amaryllis turned around. Michelle stood with a tear-stained face and she could hardly get her words out.

"I need a maid of honor for this Saturday. Do you know anyone who may be interested?"

Amaryllis immediately dropped her bag and ran into her sister's arms. The boarding clerk approached Amaryllis and tapped her shoulder. "Excuse me, Miss, that was the last call. You must board the plane."

Michelle took Amaryllis' ticket from her hand and gave it to the boarding clerk. "She's not boarding this plane. Can you change the date of this ticket to next Sunday?"

At first, the airline refused to unload Amaryllis' baggage because it would delay the plane. Amaryllis finally got to see her big sister do her thang. After Michelle clowned in the airport and threatened to sue, Amaryllis' baggage was released and brought to her feet.

Outside, the two sisters were greeted by a white stretch limousine. The driver opened the back door for them and Michelle got in first.

When Amaryllis stepped in, she saw both Nicholas and James seated. "What's going on?" Amaryllis asked.

"Daddy's taking us all out to dinner."

Amaryllis looked at her father. "Thank you, Daddy."

Nicholas smiled. "You're welcome, Baby Girl."

For years, Amaryllis longed to be acknowledged by her father and Michelle was glad that he'd finally given her the right nickname. Amaryllis looked at James. What could she possibly say that would make things right between them? She would just have to speak from her heart. "James, I don't know what to say that could make up for what I've done to you. There really are no words that would express how sorry I am."

On the seat next to James lay a dozen roses. He picked up the bouquet and gave them to her. "This is a day of new beginnings, Amaryllis, so I want to present these roses to the second most beautiful woman in the world."

Amaryllis remembered what happened the last time James called her beautiful and gave her a rose. She also knew what he meant by *new beginnings*: their friendship.

Two weeks after Amaryllis had returned from Las Vegas, she and Bridgette were on their way home after putting in twelve hours at the law firm. Amaryllis was grateful her position as an administrative assistant was still available after three months. Truly God had covered her completely. They were at a stop light on Bomer Avenue when Amaryllis looked to her left and saw Holy Deliverance Baptist Church. She thought of Randall and wondered if he was inside. She remembered that Monday nights were men's ministry at the church.

"Bridgette, turn right and park."

Bridgette looked at her. "For what?"

"I wanna see if Black is in the church. There's something I need to do."

Bridgette thought Amaryllis was up to her old tricks. "Amaryllis, you've finally gotten your life together. Why do you wanna start some mess? The man is happily married with a family."

"Will you just turn and park this car?"

Bridgette reluctantly parked and Amaryllis got out of the car. She entered the church and walked through the sanctuary door. Randall was standing facing her, talking to about fifty men and boys. He saw her face and stopped in mid-sentence. Everyone turned to see what had captured his attention and saw a beautiful woman. He motioned for a deacon to come to him. "Deacon Jones, can you take over for me?"

Randall walked out into the vestibule and stood in front of her. "Hi."

"Hey, how are you?" Amaryllis asked nervously. She wanted to turn and run out of the church, but now that she was there, she had to execute what she came to do.

"Fine, thanks. What brings you by?"

"Bridgette and I were on our way home from work and I saw the church and thought about you. I just wanted to stop in and say hello."

"Well, I'm glad you did. It's been what, about a year and a half since I've seen you? You look beautiful, as usual."

Amaryllis looked at the man she had once shared a home with for two years. He was even more handsome than she remembered. Marriage looked good on him. "You look good too, Black. Husbandhood certainly agrees with you."

Randall smiled. "Now, there's a name I haven't heard in a while. You're the only one who's ever called me that."

"Well, you'll always be Black to me."

Randall stared at Amaryllis and noticed something different about her mannerism and character, but he couldn't quite put his finger on what it was.

"Why are you looking at me like I'm an abstract art painting?" Amaryllis asked after noticing Randall's stare.

"There's something different about you."

Amaryllis was hoping Randall could see her light shining before she told him her good news. "What do you mean?"

"I don't know, it's like you're glowing or something."

Amaryllis smiled and she couldn't hold it in any longer. "Black, I've got a testimony, a confession, an apology and a request."

At the word *testimony*, Randall's eyebrows shot up in the air. "A testimony? What do you know about testifying, Amaryllis?"

"I'm getting ready to tell you. Recently, I was visiting my sister, Michelle, in Las Vegas when something happened to me that almost killed me. I was in a coma for a few hours and the doctors thought I wasn't gonna pull through."

"I'm sorry to hear that. What happened?"

"I'd rather not say, but I was doing things I had no business doing. But God touched me and woke me up."

Randall's eyebrows rose again. "What did you say?"

"I said *God* pulled me through."

Randall had to walk away from Amaryllis. He got about ten feet away then turned around and came back and stood in front of her. She was talking like a saint, and if it was one thing Randall knew about Amaryllis, it was that she was no saint. "What are you saying, Amaryllis?"

"I'm saying that in Las Vegas, I got saved and sanctified, Black. That's my testimony."

Randall's mouth dropped wide open. "Are you serious?"

"Yes. When I got back from Vegas, I joined Progressive Life-Giving Word Cathedral in Hillside and was baptized by Apostle Donald L. Alford. I even got Bridgette going to church with me and we both gave up gambling."

She was blowing Randall's mind, and again, he walked away from her and came back. He reached out and hugged her. "Amaryllis, that's wonderful. I always prayed that you'd come to know and love God. Welcome to the family."

"Thanks, Black. It feels good to be a part of the family. But now I have a confession."

"Okay, I'm listening."

"I don't want you to interrupt me until I'm done. This is new and hard for me, and if I stop, I don't think I'll be able to finish."

"Okay."

Amaryllis took a deep breath and let it out. "When we were living together, I was sleeping with a guy name Darryl for money. The guys that trashed your car were his posse. He set that up for me because I was mad at you for cutting off my gambling money." She studied Randall's face, but he showed no sign of anger. "I turned your cell phone off the night that young man, Brandon, came here to the church looking for you. I did that so Cordell couldn't contact you and change your mind about going with me to Veronica's house. And I erased the message he left for you. I got you drunk that night on purpose. I knew Veronica spiked the punch and I deliberately didn't tell you. So, I'm the reason you almost lost your job."

Amaryllis was bringing back serious memories. Listening to her speak of the past caused Randall to reflect back to the time when he spent an evening at her mother's house. Randall drove trains for the Chicago Transit Authority. He remembered drinking gin and juice when he thought it was punch. The next day Randall was so incoherent, he derailed a train.

Amaryllis kept looking at his face, but he didn't twinge. "A lady from Brandon's family called to tell you about his funeral arrangements, but I told her that she had the wrong Randall Loomis and to not call back, so I'm the reason you missed his funeral. And the evening that Cordell came over to take you to church, I purposely walked into the kitchen naked. I planned it that way."

At the mention of Brandon, something tugged at Randall's heart. He'd met Brandon on a train one morning and befriended him. Randall didn't know at that time that Brandon was troubled. The day Randall met Brandon, he invited him to men's night. But because Amaryllis threw a hissy fit about Randall spending too much time at church and not enough quality time with her, Randall didn't keep his word with Brandon. When Brandon arrived at the church that evening, Randall was nowhere to be found. Because Brandon felt that Randall had stood him up, he left the church despondent. Brandon had lost one of his jobs earlier that day and when he got home, he found his three younger siblings had been removed from their home by DCFS. And to make matters worse, Brandon found his mother dead.

The next morning, Randall read in the newspaper that Brandon was found dead due to a single gunshot wound to the head. At the time, the police assumed it was suicide. Randall felt responsible for Brandon's death and his family's misfortune. He got himself together and left Amaryllis alone for good. Randall met and married a lady named Gabrielle who was barren. Together, Randall and Gabrielle adopted Brandon's younger siblings and were now living a happy and fulfilled life.

Randall was cool as a cucumber and Amaryllis couldn't believe how calm he was.

"There were times when your mother called for you and I didn't tell you because I didn't want you talking to her." Amaryllis saved this bomb for last because she thought it would send Randall over the edge. But still he showed no emotion. "I'm done, Black."

Randall was extremely calm. "Okay."

"Okay? That's all you have to say?"

"What's there *to* say, Amaryllis?"

"I don't know, but say something. I just confessed to everything I've done to hurt you. Don't you wanna yell or something?"

"Nope. What purpose would that serve?"

"Well, I'm sorry, Black. I'm sorry for gambling, for prostituting my body, for cheating on you, for destroying the expensive Bible you bought me, for keeping you away from your mother, for all the lies I told you, for going to church with you and acting like a fool, for putting Cordell in awkward positions, for jeopardizing your health and job, for causing you not to be the mentor you needed to be for Brandon, for taking your furniture and selling it, for making you feel bad about going to church, for taking your love for granted, for not appreciating you the way I should have and for not being the woman you needed me to be."

By the time Amaryllis was done apologizing, her face was streaked with mascara. Randall was messed up too. For so long, he had prayed that Amaryllis would come to a point of maturity and take responsibility for her actions. Even after they separated, he had continued praying for her.

He wiped tears from his own eyes. "You said you had a request, what is it?"

With the history she and Randall shared, Amaryllis knew she had no right to ask this of him, but she couldn't leave this church and go on with her life until Randall released her. "I need you to forgive me, Black; for everything."

Randall pulled her into his arms and hugged her. "Amaryllis, everything you just confessed to, I already knew. You were forgiven a long time ago."

It felt good to be in his arms again and this time, unadulterated. "Thanks, Black. I needed to hear that."

"You're welcome, Precious."

She looked up at him. "What did you call me?" Amaryllis asked stunned that he had referred to her by the nickname he'd given her.

"You'll always be Precious to me," Randall smiled.

They looked at each other and held a smile, then Amaryllis pulled away. "I should be going. You need to get back to your session and Bridgette's outside waiting."

She turned and walked toward the door. When she put her hand on the doorknob, Randall called out to her. "Precious, can I give you some advice before you go?"

"Sure, Black, what is it?"

"Now that you are a part of God's family, He wants to use you for His glory. Let Him do it. He's getting ready to turn your life upside down and inside out. It won't always feel good, but the outcome is well worth the growing pains. There are gonna be times when the enemy will come at you so strong that you won't know what hit you. But I promise you that if you keep your face in God's face, He'll protect you.

"Whatever is in your past should remain in your past. It doesn't matter what you did before you decided to trust God with your life. He's forgiven you and it's important that you forgive yourself, because if you don't do that, you'll always beat yourself up over what's in the past. Understand that God has started your life over with a clean slate, so live it to its fullest."

Randall walked closer to Amaryllis and looked her in her eyes. "Beware of destiny preventers and dream killers. Folks are going to come to you and remind you of the things you used to do. Just know that they are working for the enemy and are trying to make you think that you're not worthy of God's love. No matter what anybody says or throws in your face, know in your heart that you are now a child of the King.

"And don't be afraid of trials. Learn to expect them because they will definitely come. It's how you handle them that makes all the difference. Remember that you have the power of the Holy Ghost to help you through anything. I encourage you to stay in the Word of God because it's your weapon. Make sure you read it daily. And lastly, never, ever, under any circumstances, underestimate how low the enemy will go to destroy you. He's smart and always on top of his game. He knows your weaknesses and will come at you from every angle. Stay alert at all times and never turn your back on him because he's not to be trusted. Remember to keep your friends close and your enemies closer. Keep in mind that God protects you from all hurt, harm and danger. And tell yourself everyday that with God, you can make it through anything."

Amaryllis was outdone. She felt like this was a sermon written just for her. She had come full circle. "Thanks, Black. Those words will stay with me forever."

She walked out of the church and was going down the steps toward Bridgette's car when the church's neon sign lit up and she stopped to read it.

Holy Deliverance Baptist Church
Bishop Cordell Bryson, *Pastor*
Minister/Elder Randall Loomis, *Assistant Pastor*

Minister, Elder, Assistant Pastor? Amaryllis was surprised and she wondered when Randall had been called into ministry. She turned around and saw Randall standing at the top of the church steps smiling at her.

She returned his smile, then walked down the church's steps and out of Randall's life with a determination to stay on the right path.

Reader's Group Guide Questions

1. In the previous novel, *A Man's Worth*, Amaryllis was prejudiced against marriage. In this novel, how do you think seeing Randall and his new bride, affected Amaryllis?

2. Amaryllis's father, Nicholas, had a strong dislike for her. Why?

3. Why did Michelle dismiss their father's warnings about her sister?

4. A sister's fiancé' is off limits. What do you think it was about James that made Amaryllis break this unspoken rule?

5. Do you think James made a mistake when he presented Amaryllis with a rose the first time he met her? If so, why? If not, why?

6. Amaryllis appeared before James in the nude. Against his pastor's advice, he chose not to trust in the love that Michelle had for him to tell her. If James had, in fact, shared with Michelle her sister's evil ways, do you think Michelle would have believed him?

7. Nicholas had seen, with his own eyes, James's face in the puzzle. Why was he still protecting James?

8. When the truth about what Amaryllis had done to James was revealed to Michelle, was it wrong for her

to punch Amaryllis in the nose and send her packing?

9. After all of the grief Amaryllis had caused her, why did Michelle sit at Amaryllis's death bed and pray her out of the coma?

10. Why did Amaryllis confess to Randall all of her wrongdoings in their relationship?

She's back . . . and trying to stay saved!

Amaryllis Price returns in Nikita Lynnette Nichols's
forthcoming novel:

CROSSROADS

An excerpt

*The chauffer pulled up to the curb at 743 Woodland
Street, Baton Rouge, Louisiana.*

Amaryllis looked at Michelle. "You ready?"

*Michelle's stomach was doing flip-flops. She'd rather
not face the unknown. "I've changed my mind. I don't
wanna find out what happened to us. Let's just go back
to the hotel."*

*Amaryllis moved next to Michelle and hugged her.
"You know we need answers. This is what we came all
the way to Louisiana for."*

*Michelle looked at her husband with pity in her eyes.
"Honey, please say a prayer before we go in."*

*After James's prayer, the two couples found them-
selves standing on the front porch. Charles had a tight
grip on Amaryllis's hand. Because Michelle appeared to
need much more moral support than Amaryllis, James
held her tightly by the waist.*

Amaryllis exhaled, rang the doorbell, and looked at

her sister. "*This is it, Michelle. There's no turning back now.*"

"*I gotta throw up,*" Michelle said.

An overweight, gray haired woman opened the door. She looked at the four of them in their faces, but she concentrated most on the two women.

Amaryllis was the first to speak. "*Hi, Nana.*"

Nana placed her left hand on her heart. "*Oh, my God. Oh, Jesus.*" She looked from Amaryllis to Michelle then from Michelle to Amaryllis. "*Oh, sweet Jesus. I can't believe you're here. Come in, come in.*"

Amaryllis stepped into the living room and Charles followed. Michelle's feet were planted on the front porch, she didn't have the nerve to place one foot ahead of the other. James nudged her back to get her moving.

Amaryllis walked to her grandmother and embraced her. "*It's good to see you, Nana.*"

Nana returned the hug. "*You too, baby.*"

Amaryllis held her hand out for Michelle to grab. "*Nana, this is my sister, Michelle.*"

Seeing Michelle for the first time caused tears to fall onto Nana's cheeks. She held her arms open for Michelle.

Michelle released Amaryllis's hand and slowly walked to Nana and hugged her. "*It's nice to meet you, Nana.*"

Amaryllis motioned for James and Charles to come closer to where she, Michelle and their grandmother stood. "*Nana, I want you to meet James, Michelle's husband, and my friend, Charles.*"

James and Charles greeted Nana and kissed her on opposite cheeks.

Nana looked at them all. "*Sit down, please. Why didn't you tell me you were coming? I would've prepared a feast.*"

Amaryllis and Charles, along with Michelle and James, squeezed themselves on a sofa opposite of Nana.

Amaryllis spoke. "Because, this is sort of a spur of the moment thing, Nana. Michelle and I came here for answers."

Nana eyed Amaryllis in confusion. "Answers?"

"When I asked you to send me my birth certificate, I received Michelle's instead."

Nana's face turned crimson red. "Oh, my goodness. I don't know how I could've made that mistake. I've always been so careful."

"What is there to be careful about?" Michelle asked confused, not sure if she really wanted to know the answer to her own question.

"About keeping your parents' secret," Nana confessed. "But I guess the secret is out now, since you're here."

Amaryllis scooted to the edge of her seat. "That's right, Nana. And we want you to tell us why we were raised to believe that we were three years apart and had different mothers."

"Has either of you asked your parents?" was Nana's reply.

"Amaryllis doesn't talk to her mother, Veronica, and our father is away on vacation. But he told me that my mother had died when I was about six months old," Michelle said.

"Nana, we came here for answers, that at the moment, only you can give. Don't turn us away," Amaryllis pleaded.

Nana looked at her granddaughters' faces. How could she deny them their right to know their history, their roots? "I don't know where to begin."

"At the beginning," Amaryllis replied.

So that she wouldn't miss one word out of Nana's mouth,

Michelle scooted to the edge of the sofa like Amaryllis. "My birth certificate states we were born in November of 1974. You can go back nine months prior and begin there."

Nana leaned back in her rocker, crossed her ankles, and exhaled. "Your father, Nicholas, came to Baton Rouge to attend a week long realtor's convention. One evening, he, along with a colleague, visited a bar. My daughter, Veronica, tended the bar. She fell for Nicholas the moment she saw him. According to Veronica, she and Nicholas became friendly with one another. The more drinks she served him, the friendlier he became. He invited Veronica out for dinner the next evening and she graciously accepted.

"Over dinner, Nicholas told Veronica that he lived in Chicago and made a lot of money selling houses. Money has always been Veronica's god. After dinner with Nicholas, Veronica was smitten. She wanted to make him fall in love with her. But Nicholas would only be in town for two more days, so she had to work fast. Veronica asked me to help her and I did."

"How did you help her, Nana?" Amaryllis asked.

"I put a root on Nicholas."

Michelle's jaw dropped. James and Charles looked at each other and frowned at what Nana had just said.

"A root?" Amaryllis asked.

"What's a root?" Charles asked Nana. Even though he was there as a silent partner, to only support Amaryllis, he was drawn into the conversation. He blurted out the question without thinking.

Nana shifted in her recliner. "A root is a spell, black magic, voodoo, black art, hocus-pocus, sorcery, it's all the same."

"But that's witchcraft," James volunteered.

Nana looked at James. "It's what I do, honey. Creole women have been practicing witchcraft for generations. My grandmother was a witch, my mother was a witch. I'm a witch. My daughter, Veronica, is a witch. Amaryllis and Michelle are witches too. We're all witches. And any offspring from this bloodline will be wizards and witches as well."

Michelle vomited on the floor in front of her. She hadn't yet shared with James that she may be pregnant.

Bio

Nikita Lynnette Nichols is the author of *None But The Righteous* and *A Man's Worth*.
She makes her home in Naperville, Illinois, and is currently writing her next novel.

You can reach the author at:
nikitalynnettenichols.com or
kitawrites@comcast.net

Urban Christian His Glory Book Club!

Established January 2007, *UC His Glory Book Club* is another way by which to introduce to the literary world Urban Books' much-anticipated new imprint, **Urban Christian** and its authors. We are an online book club supporting Urban Christian authors by purchasing, reading and providing written reviews of the authors' books that are read. *UC His Glory* welcomes both men and women of the literary world who have a passion for reading Christian-based fiction.

UC His Glory is the brainchild of Joylynn Jossel, Author and Executive Editor of Urban Christian and Kendra Norman-Bellamy, Author and Copy Editor for Urban Christian. The book club will provide support, positive feedback, encouragement and a forum whereby members can openly discuss and review the literary works of Urban Christian authors. In the future, we anticipate broadening our spectrum of services to include online author chats, author spotlights, interviews with your favorite Urban Christian author(s), special online groups for *UC His Glory Book Club* members, ability to post reviews on the website and amazon.com, membership ID cards, *UC His Glory* Yahoo Group and much more.

Even though there will be no membership fees attached to becoming a member of *UC His Glory Book Club*, we do expect our members to be active, committed and to follow the guidelines of the book club.

UC His Glory members pledge to:

- Follow the guidelines of *UC His Glory Book Club*.
- Provide input, opinions, and reviews that build up, rather than tear down.
- Commit to purchasing, reading and discussing featured book(s) of the month.
- Agree not to miss more than three consecutive online monthly meetings.
- Respect the Christian beliefs of *UC His Glory Book Club*.
- Believe that Jesus is the Christ, Son of the Living God

We look forward to the online fellowship.

Many Blessings to You!

Shelia E. Lipsey
President
UC His Glory Book Club

**Visit the official Urban Christian His Glory Book Club website at *www.uchisglorybookclub.net*